THE HIDDEN

KIERSTEN MODGLIN

Cover Design by Kiersten Modglin
Copy Editing by Three Owls Editing
Proofreading by My Brother's Editor
Formatting & Graphic Design by Kiersten Modglin

First Print and Electronic Edition: 2024
kierstenmodglinauthor.com

To the ones shining light in the darkest corners—
the fighters
the hopers
the givers
the slayers of our most terrifying monsters

CHAPTER ONE

5—4:23:58

I have no idea where I am. It's a terrifying realization every single time it happens, and yet here I am once again. My eyes feel like sandpaper when I try to open them—dry and painful as I stare into the light shining through.

I roll over, my body stiff, and the movement is enough to cause my stomach to heave.

I'm going to throw up.

I'm going to throw up.

I'm going to throw up.

With the sudden agility of a child, I jolt up from the bed, moving quickly in search of a bathroom in a space I don't recognize. I can't focus on that right now, can't question where I ended up after another night of drinking.

With singular focus and only seconds to spare, I pull open one of three doors in the room and find an

1

empty closet—a few unused plastic hangers dangling on the metal bar. I move to the next door and shove it open, vomit already in my throat.

I'm not going to make it.

There's no way I'll make it.

I have to make it.

If I open my mouth, I'm going to spew everywhere.

Relieved doesn't feel like a strong enough word for what I feel when my eyes land on a toilet in the small, dark room. I launch myself onto the floor and empty the contents of my stomach, my body shaking, head throbbing.

I hate this. I hate this. I hate this.

The morning after is never the most enjoyable part of a date, but I'd prefer not to throw up in front of the person who saw me naked last night if given the choice.

When my stomach feels completely empty, the anxiety and dread begin to take over. The embarrassment over my situation—over everything my date just heard in here and the scent I've just filled this bathroom with—seeps into my organs, and I can think of nothing else.

I wipe my mouth. My skin seems to be throbbing like a pulse, every muscle tense and thrumming. The bathroom is small but pristine. *Must be a guest bathroom. I know* my *bathroom has never been this clean.*

Then again, I guess we could be in a hotel, although

the place feels more like an apartment or condo than any hotel room I've ever been in.

Everything is bright white, like a movie version of heaven. There's not a single bottle of body wash or shampoo behind the white plastic shower curtain, nor is there anything except a new bar of soap on the countertop next to the sink. I rinse my mouth by filling my palm with water, then wash my hands as I examine myself in the mirror. I recognize the clothes I'm wearing from my closet—my favorite jeans and a purple shirt—but I don't recall putting them on.

I'm exhausted. That's what sticks with me the most. Despite just sleeping for what feels like a century, fatigue clings to my bones and muscles like a claw clip in my hair, its spindly fingers wrapped around my body in a vise-like grip.

I slurp down another handful of water before making my way back into the bedroom, listening for the sounds of whoever else might be in this apartment with me. Will they be the type to make breakfast? Or pick up breakfast? Or will I find a note on the counter telling me to let myself out without even being able to remember the face of the person I spent my night with?

The bedroom, like the bathroom, is nondescript. Sterile nearly. The bed frame is plain, black metal, and the bed set is simple and white. I don't have to look closer to know it's cheap and scratchy to the skin, though I don't remember my night here to confirm it. There are no photos on the walls or memorabilia of any kind. There's not even a TV. The room is a completely blank slate. A white box.

Suddenly, claustrophobia takes hold of my throat, making it hard to swallow. I can't seem to get enough oxygen in here.

I force out a slow, steady breath, trying to think. To prepare myself before I walk out there and re-meet my date.

A man, I'm guessing. The lack of decorations feels like a dead giveaway that this room doesn't belong to a woman, though I've never seen a man's room this tidy either. I'm utterly baffled at how I ended up in this white box without a single memory of last night.

I'm still listening for sounds, though I'm pretty convinced I'm alone since no one came to check on me during my not-silent vomit session moments ago. Either that, or whoever I slept with is a total asshole and can't be bothered to care.

Way to pick 'em, Sophie.

I can practically hear Jaz chastising me from wherever she is. Maybe I won't tell her about this one. I definitely won't tell her.

Crossing the room, I ease down onto my knees and search the nightstand and under the bed for my purse and phone. I need to find out where I am, call an Uber, and get home in time to not miss my entire shift at The Bold Bean. *Margie's going to kill me.*

Hell, Simon's going to kill me. His bowl of food is probably empty by now, and I'm sure he's currently meowing at me through the abyss, which is only going to make Jaz mad, and then *she's* going to kill me.

I'm dead times three, and I have no idea where my phone is.

Fucking fuck.

I must've left it in the living room when we came inside. God help me if I left it at the bar. I don't even remember which one we were at. Or who *we* entails.

Oh my god, I have got to stop drinking. Never again. I will never do this again.

With a deep breath, I prepare for the utmost embarrassment as I walk out of the bedroom and down a short hallway into the small kitchen on my right. It's narrow with a peninsula and, like every other room here, completely, blindingly white.

"Hello?" I call, my voice scratchy. The apartment is silent as I study the faded beige couch in the living room next to the kitchen. There's no television in here either, but I spot a small shelf of old books in the corner. My purse and phone are nowhere to be seen.

Chills line my arms as I spin back around, checking over my shoulder. The curtains are pulled closed, and if it hadn't been for the light in the bedroom telling me it was morning, it could easily pass for the middle of the night. My eyes trail the walls until they land on a black box that runs the full length of the wall across from the couch. Almost like a mini split air conditioner, but much longer.

I have no idea what it is and have never seen anything like it before.

I check the couch cushions next, but like everything else, it's surprisingly clean. No sign of my purse, phone, or a single crumb. Whoever lives here would probably feel the need to wear a hazmat suit in my apartment.

Tears prickle my eyes at the idea of abandoning my stuff. How am I supposed to call an Uber or reach out to anyone if I don't have a phone? Not to mention the risk of identity theft and credit card fraud now that god knows who has my wallet.

Never ever again.

I'm so angry with myself. Still, I don't see what choice I have. Whoever lives here could be gone for hours for all I know, and I don't even know for certain that my purse made it back here.

I don't even know how I made it back here.

Lately, my life has been a string of bad decisions, but I'm usually not so irresponsible that I black out or end up in a stranger's home. With a final look around, a shift of cushions and checking of mostly empty kitchen drawers, I give a resigned sigh and make my way toward the door.

In a last-ditch attempt, I grab a napkin and fish a pen from one of the kitchen drawers, scratching down Jaz's phone number with a note that says,

If you find my things, please call.

I consider saying thank you for last night, but that feels strange considering that I have no idea how last night even went. I'm mildly sore between my legs, which tells me we probably slept together, but I don't know if it's worthy of a thank you, so I leave it at that.

With nothing else to do, I make my way to the door and grab at the handle. I twist the knob, but…it doesn't move.

Looking up, I realize the lock is on backward and I'm staring at a keyhole in the knob and a dead bolt above it. It takes several seconds for me to process this before the panic sets in.

No. No. No. No. No.

What the hell?

I jerk at the handle again and again, but it doesn't budge. I rush to the kitchen, searching for anything that might help me pick the lock. I need to get out of here. I can't breathe. Can't think. I try a knife first, stabbing it into the keyhole and twisting, but it doesn't move. The knife bends slightly, but the keyhole is entirely unaffected.

I try a pen, with less hope, and give up after seconds. Next is a fork, which works about as well as the knife, which is to say it gives me a second's hope before smashing it to bits.

I look around the room, searching for anything else that might help. When my eyes find the black box on the wall again, I do a double take. It's different now. Red digits fill the black screen.

5—4:23:58

A lump of dough lodges in my throat. What does it mean? Is it a code? Is it...some sort of alarm code? There's no keypad here. I have no idea what these numbers mean or why they just showed up.

What the fuck is going on?

I feel as if I'm on the set of some stupid sci-fi film. Oh, Jaz is going to think this is all hilarious...if I can ever find a way to get out of here and tell her.

"Hello?" I call again, my voice trembling as I stare up at the numbers. "Can anyone hear me?"

With no answer, I cross the room and open the curtains. Behind both curtains, there's a single pane of solid glass. Beyond the glass, I see only trees in every direction—no other houses, no roads, nothing.

There's no way to open the windows. I have to go through them. I have to find a way to break the glass, to damage this person's property. Could I be arrested for this? Or sued? I have no money to be sued, and I certainly don't have time to be arrested.

I picture myself on the news—my mugshot and the story of how I destroyed someone's windows because I couldn't find the back door of their house after a wild night of partying. They'll make me look insane. People will blame me for drinking too much. My parents will tell their friends I'm *going through a rough time* without ever checking in on me.

I'm not entirely sure I'm not dreaming at this point.

I don't have a choice. I need to get out of here, and there are no other doors.

Just to be sure, I walk back to the bedroom and check every door, even the one to the bathroom which I'm now very well acquainted with, but there's nothing. This door and these windows are the only way out.

I swallow, trying to slow my rapid breathing as I search for something to safely break the glass. If someone is nearby, they're almost certainly going to hear this. If that someone is the person who locked me in here, if they locked me in on purpose, I'm going to have to be fast.

That thought catches my breath, squeezing my lungs. *Someone potentially locked me in here.*

Someone brought me here.

Someone…kidnapped me?

I'm twenty-six. Not a kid, but still…stolen? Locked away? Hidden?

It doesn't feel real or possible. I know you hear the stories, and it feels cliché to say I didn't think it would happen to me, but wow. I still feel like I'm overreacting or being dramatic, and I hate that part of myself.

This is real. It's serious.

Or…it's a TikTok prank.

I swear to god…

Well, if I was kidnapped, if someone plans to hurt me, I won't go down without a fight. I'm not some silly little girl they can lock up and who won't fight back. Seriously, they don't know who they're messing with, though I suddenly wish I'd stuck with karate for more than two weeks as a kid. It was the gi. No one tells you how itchy they are.

Still searching for something to break the window with, I survey the room. The couch and the coffee table are out; they're too heavy for me to lift on my own, and there are no kitchen chairs or barstools for me to use.

Ooh.

Thinking quickly, I rush back to the bedroom and grab the nightstand, jerking it away from the wall and ignoring the lamp as it falls to the floor.

I carry it into the living room, sweat making my hair cling to the back of my neck, the taste of vomit burning my throat, and then, with all my might, I throw the nightstand directly into the window.

I feel like a badass. A fighter. Like I've really shown them I'm someone to be feared.

...And that lasts for all of three seconds.

Until I watch the nightstand hit the window and bounce off of it as if it were rubber before crashing to the ground.

I squeeze my hands into fists, turning my head toward the sky and releasing a guttural scream.

"If this is a prank, now's the time to end it!" I shout to whatever TikTok bro might be listening. "Seriously, this isn't funny!"

I brush my hair out of my face, wishing I had a hair tie. Wishing I had my purse. My phone. Wishing I had a way out of here.

I pick up the nightstand again, throwing it harder. My muscles scream from the exertion, but like before, it slams to the floor, the window completely unfazed.

I grab the nightstand and haul it back to the bedroom in a haze of fury and exhaustion. After pulling the curtains aside, I launch the nightstand into the window with all my might.

"Come on!" I bellow when the nightstand hits the floor again without leaving even a single hairline crack in the glass.

No.

No.

No.

I stare around in disbelief, then rush forward, pounding my hands on the glass of every window in the apartment, then the walls, and the door.

"Help!" I cry. "Help! Someone, please! If you can hear me, please help! I'm trapped!" My voice cracks as the realization sets in, and I step away from the door, my hands and arms throbbing.

I'm trapped.

I'm trapped.

Breathe, Sophie.

I can't breathe. I'm suffocating. There's no way out.

CHAPTER TWO

BEFORE — SEVEN YEARS AGO

She's not who I was expecting.

The door to my hospital room opens, and the woman who enters isn't dressed in scrubs. That's the first thing I notice about her. She looks out of place here in her one-piece cream jumper, with a little tie at the waist that exposes several inches of her brown skin. Her face is fresh and clean, with little makeup and just a hint of gloss on her lips.

She's stunning in the most basic way. Model pretty, with big, curly hair that forms a halo around her head.

At seeing me, she stops in her tracks, looking over her shoulder, then back at me like she's in the wrong place.

Clearly she's in the wrong place, but I don't want her to leave. *Is that weird? What kind of drugs do they have me on right now?*

Her eyes search my face, and finally, her mouth drops open. "You're not my grandma."

A corner of my mouth lifts with a smile I can't help. "I feel like I'm supposed to tell you my big eyes are better to see you with or something like that."

She pauses, processing, and I'm officially an idiot. "Was that a 'Little Red Riding Hood' joke?"

"Probably." I reach for the pudding on my tray, and her eyes flash to the bandages around my wrists. I drop my hands quickly, heat rising in my chest.

She seems hesitant, like she's going to bolt at any second, but to my surprise, she stays in place. "Is this room four twenty-three?"

"Close." I pick at the paper on my pudding, trying and failing to open it. "Four twenty-one."

She takes a step back. "Shoot, I'm sorry. I was looking for my grandma. She's next door."

I wince as pain shoots through my arm and place the pudding cup back on the tray. "It's okay. No worries."

She turns to the door, and my heart sinks. I want to stop her, to finally have someone to talk to, but what can I say that won't make me seem utterly pathetic?

To my surprise, she stops in her tracks, turning back to me. "Do you…need some help with that?" She gestures toward the pudding cup, and I feel like a toddler as I nod.

"That would be nice. Thanks."

Slowly, already looking as if she regrets it, she inches toward me.

"I'm Sophie, by the way," I tell her.

Her eyes flick up to meet mine. "I'm Jasmine. Jaz."

"Jaz." I let the word roll over my tongue as she tears open the pudding cup and places it back down in front of me.

"Thank you." I lift it slowly, stabbing my plastic spoon into the chocolate mush.

She nods, lips pressed together, and takes a step back. "I should let you get back to..." Her words trail off as she eyes the television, which is on a commercial about a local law firm that I've already seen a billion times today.

"Thanks," I tell her. "It's riveting stuff, really."

She smiles softly. Awkwardly.

"I hope your grandma's okay."

That seems to surprise her. "Oh. Thanks. She's..." Her mouth twists, and I get the feeling she's trying not to cry. "She's not, really."

"Oh. Sorry. I shouldn't have said anything."

"It's fine," she says, her words overlapping mine.

We both chuckle, and I push a second, unopened pudding cup at her. "Normally, I'd offer to buy you a drink and talk about it, but pudding is all I have to offer." I grin at her. "Wanna have a cup with me?"

She hesitates.

"Feel free to tell me to buzz off. Though...I guess you'd be the one buzzing away, since I'm stuck here."

She laughs then, and it's warm. It lights up her whole face. "No. I appreciate it, but I'm vegan, so I can't."

I stare down at the pudding in my hand, feeling like a glutton. "Oh. Sorry. I, um…"

"It's fine," she assures me, sitting down in the chair next to the bed. "Really. Actually"—she reaches into her purse and pulls out a bag of lightly salted green pea chips—"I brought snacks, and I'd love to join you for a little bit. My grandma usually naps around this time anyway."

The relief that floods through me as she sits down isn't normal. Then again, I've been in this room for a week with no visitors except for the doctors and nurses, so I guess it just feels good to have someone here who isn't being paid to check on me.

"I don't want to keep you from her," I say, though I *really, really* do, selfish as that may be.

"I'm already snacking." She tears open her bag. "Can't eat and walk. That'd be a choking hazard." With a wide grin, she pops a chip into her mouth.

"Those look terrible," I admit, then instantly regret the words.

Her face is stoic for a moment, then tilts into a smile. "They're actually really good." She holds the bag out, and I'm tempted to reach for one, just to be nice, but when I lift my hand, the stiffness of the bandage reminds me it's there, and I pull it back down.

"Thanks, but I'll take your word for it."

"Suit yourself," she teases, keeping the mood light. "So where is your usual pudding-opener?"

"The nurse comes in about every hour," I tell her. "I was sleeping when they brought these."

She starts to put a chip in her mouth but stops. "I meant whoever you have visiting you. Family or friends…" I can see the moment the answer to her question registers on her face, and her smile fades.

"Is this a good time to tell you I am, in fact, the big bad wolf, and I ate them all already?"

Her lips press together with a small smile, and she shakes her head. "It's the perfect time. Since I have an ax in my bag and nothing to do today except save mankind."

"What are the odds?" I ask with a laugh. I've never been someone with a lot of friends, or any friends really, but somehow, in this moment, she's exactly what I needed.

"What are the odds?" She keeps her gaze trained on my face, like she's trying to figure me out, but somehow I don't mind. As long as she stays right here with me, I don't mind at all.

CHAPTER THREE

5—4:20:05

I pace. And scream. And shout. And pound on the walls and windows over and over again, hoping with everything in me that a neighbor might hear the sound and either investigate or call for help. I throw things at windows and stick everything that will fit into the keyholes, trying desperately to find my way out of here. *How did I end up here anyway?*

The more I think about it, the more it terrifies me. I have no way to contact anyone. No way to call Jaz.

I bang my hands against the walls, screaming and praying for someone to hear me, but if they do, no one answers. No one comes for me.

I'm alone and terrified and trapped.

Finally, when I've exhausted myself to the point of nearly passing out, I sink down on the floor in the living room. The red numbers on the wall now read:

5—4:20:05

It's a countdown, I realize. A countdown for four days from now, I think, but what happens then? And what does the five mean? The fridge is completely empty. I have water, at least, from the sink, but will I even survive four days locked in here without food? Will I want to?

I have to get home. Jaz deserves to know what happened to me. I can't leave her wondering forever. She'll take care of Simon, I know that. She'll have woken up by now, realized I'm not back, and fed him. How long will it take her to begin to wonder why I'm still not home?

How long until she tries to call me, if she hasn't already? How long until she calls my parents or checks in at the coffee shop? When will the panic set in?

I hate that this will become her problem. I hate that she'll be the one to have to search for me, but if anyone will do it, if anyone *can* do it, it's Jaz. She'll start putting the pieces together, figure out who I was with last night, where I went. She'll demand to see security footage, and they'll let her because no one says no to Jaz. She'll save me, but I can't wait for her.

I won't be that girl.

I won't sit around and wait for a knight in shining—sustainably sourced—armor.

If there's a way out of this room, even if I have to burrow out with a spoon into the drywall, I will. I will not stay here and wait to die. Wait to find out why they have me here in the first place and who *they* are.

I stand up, crossing the room and grabbing a knife from the drawer. I'm not weaponless, at least. If someone comes for me, I'll be ready. As ready as I can be.

I wish I could remember something about yesterday, assuming that's when I was brought here, but my mind is a blurry mess of fog and confusion. There are pieces there—I remember cuddling with Simon in bed, running my hands through his fur while he purred, waiting for his breakfast. I remember getting breakfast with Jaz at that little brunch place she loves before work, but even work is sort of blurry. I'm almost positive I was there, but I don't remember talking to customers or any of my coworkers.

I hate this.

I hate that I have no idea what happened to me. I have no idea how much time has passed. The only logical explanation for this is that I was drugged, but that's difficult to swallow.

I've always been careful with my drinks and food, but clearly I messed up. Girls aren't allowed to make mistakes like looking away from their drinks for a split second. I've known this. Jaz drilled it into my head every night before I left the apartment. I knew. I knew. I knew, and I still slipped up.

I'll never forgive myself if I don't make it out of this. It's one thing to know someone had bad intentions—

there are bad people out there. It's a fact of life. But I've always been careful. I've always been aware.

And still, I'm here.

And god knows where *here* even is.

I could be in another city or state. Another country even.

I walk to the window and peer out again. Like I suspected earlier, as far as I can tell, the apartment is completely surrounded by a thick forest. From what I can see, there's nothing defining here, just trees. They look somewhat local, I guess. Like, there are no trees that look completely foreign to me, but then again, how would I know? They're trees.

I'm losing my mind.

The building I'm in is low to the ground, so it's possible it's a house, though the size and fixtures make it feel more like a cheap apartment. I can't see any other buildings around, nor any cars or roads. It's as if I'm completely alone here, like the apartment was dropped out in the middle of the woods and forgotten about.

Thinking back to my original, insane plan, I return to the kitchen and grab a spoon. Could I actually dig myself out of here somehow? Probably not, but I want to try.

I need to stay busy, or I'm going to have a heart attack.

I sit down on the floor next to the couch and use the spoon to poke at the drywall, but only a small chip of the white paint comes off. I do it again, pushing harder this time as I break into the chalky surface. It's a slow and painstaking process as I dig, wiggling the spoon this way and that to clear a small dent in the wall. I knew it would be hard, but I never thought it would be this bad. Fifteen minutes in, and I've just barely broken through the tiniest section, nowhere near big enough to fit a finger in, let alone my entire body.

A sound outside the door draws my attention, snapping me out of my pity party and exhaustion. I jump up, wiping sweat from my forehead and drywall dust from my hands. I back up against the opposite wall, heart racing in my chest.

Is this the moment where I find out this has all been a prank? Or where my date comes home and asks why I'm destroying his house? Or is this the moment when I meet my fate? Where I'm attacked or killed?

I need to think quickly. The knife is still on the floor. I dart over and scoop up the weapon, my fingers wrapping around the handle as I steel myself, preparing for the worst. If the door opens, it may be one of the only chances I have to escape, which means I'll have to fight for my life to get out.

I hold my breath, creeping to hide behind the counter in the kitchen as I hear someone whistling outside. I'm going to come face to face with my captor, finally going to get answers.

The door opens, and I press my lips together, listening.

This is it.

Everything changes right now.

The person enters slowly. I can't see them, but I hear the noise of their shoes shuffling across the linoleum. They shut the door and the lock clicks. My heart sinks. When they finally come into view, they're dressed all in black, including a face covering, with only a small, glassy, iridescent shield over their eyes. They're taller than I am, but average build. I think it's a man, but the thick nylon armor makes it impossible to say for sure. They're dressed like a ninja in the most terrifying way. In their covered hands, they're holding a box. I'm scared to know what's inside.

They're looking for me. I watch their head swivel to the right and left, and I know that they're going to turn around seconds before they do.

When they turn, we find ourselves staring at each other. I stand to my full height, huffing a breath. It's hard to read them without being able to see their face. I can't tell if they're smiling or glaring. I can't tell if it's someone I know or a complete stranger.

I thought I'd fight. Attack. Instead, I want answers.

"What do you want from me?"

The person sets the cardboard box on the counter slowly, their hands going up.

"Put down the knife, Sophie." The voice is muffled, but it definitely belongs to a man.

"No." I lift it up, keeping it close to my shoulder, pointed at him. "Not until you let me out of here."

"I can't do that," he says, clasping his hands in front of him.

"Let me out of here, or I'll stab you." My voice trembles, betraying me. I never thought I'd have to say those words. How is this my life now?

"You know why you're here, Sophie. You know we can't let you go."

"What the hell are you talking about?"

Now ignoring the knife, ignoring me, he opens the box and reaches inside. I step back as he pulls out a platter of deli meat and cheese, then an apple. He places the food on the counter before retrieving a bag of chips and a cookie.

"I'll be back with more tomorrow, so make this last the day, okay?" He pulls a stack of small boxes out of the big box—puzzles like my granny used to do.

"What is going on?" I ask, my voice catching in my throat. "None of this makes any sense. Who are you? Where am I?"

He closes the lid of the box and picks it up, tucking it up against his side. "Who I am doesn't matter. You are somewhere safe. I'm here to help you." He gestures toward the food. "Eat. Drink. Rest."

He nods, then steps back and toward the door. As he reaches it, I see my chance, and I can't hesitate or second-guess. This is it. I seize my opportunity with both hands. I launch forward, running at him with the knife in the air. He turns back just in time for the knife to hit him square in the shoulder. But hitting him is all it does. The blade can't penetrate the thick, nylon fabric of his body armor. It hits, but stops. With the impact, my hand slides dangerously close to the blade. He stares at me, though I can't see his eyes through the glass, then places his hands on my shoulders to nudge me backward.

"I'll be back," he says simply. "Please don't try that again."

When he opens the door, it's only enough for him to slip out. I stare down at the knife in my hand as I hear the door being locked from the outside.

How did this happen?

I was on a date.

I went on a date yesterday.

The thought hits me in my current state of stupor, but I can't remember who my date was. I can't remember what they looked like. Like the man in black, their memory is just a shadow, and I have yet to find a source of light strong enough to see them.

CHAPTER FOUR

BEFORE — SEVEN YEARS AGO

When the door to my hospital room opens, I look up, expecting to see my nurse, who promised to return any minute with my discharge paperwork. Instead, my smile grows wide at the sight of Jaz's bright orange tank top and flowy, graphic pants.

"Well, hey you," she says, eyes wide. "Nice to see you out of bed."

"And dressed." I wave my hands over the olive green sweat suit the nurse brought me this morning. It's far from fashionable, and I refuse to think about why the hospital has it, but at this point, anything is better than the hospital gown I've been wearing for the past several days.

"Hot stuff," Jaz says with a wink. "You didn't tell me they were releasing you when I was here last."

Since her accidental visit, Jaz has stopped by my room nearly every day when she comes to visit her grandma. Neither of us has spoken about it, and it hasn't been planned, she's just done it, and it has meant everything to me.

But now…what? What does this mean? I'm leaving today and the hard reality is that I might not see her again. For all I know, she's been visiting me out of guilt because she's here anyway, but will have no desire to see me again after this is all over.

For all I know, she'll be relieved not to have to visit me anymore.

"They just told me yesterday," I admit, clasping my hands together as I ease down on the bed. "Listen, I should've already said this, but thanks for, you know, visiting me these past few days. And being my designated snack opener."

She gives a soft laugh. "Well, I was just using the pudding cups as an excuse to catch up on *Grace and Frankie* with you."

With you.

Those two words send a zing of electricity through me, though I'm not sure she meant them in any way that matters. We're still surface-level. A few hours spent watching TV and snacking over the past couple of days doesn't mean anything.

Except…maybe it does.

"Well, I'm glad you did. Seriously. I, um, I'm not used to having people I can count on." I clear my throat. "And that makes me sound about as pathetic as it gets, so I'm just going to shut up now and say thank you again. And I hope your grandma gets better." I give a slow tilt of my head, dipping my chin to meet my chest like I'm...bowing? *What the hell is wrong with me? I've been in this room too long.*

She crosses the room toward me quickly, one hand on her hip. "Why are you acting like this is goodbye?"

"Oh. I just thought..."

"I know what you thought," she says firmly, lips pursed. "You thought I was just coming around to be nice. Well, I hate to break it to you, Soph, but I'm not a nice person. I'm really mean, in fact." She grimaces. "So...I guess you're, like, stuck with me now."

It takes me a second to work out if she's joking, but then she pulls me into a quick hug. "Alright, come on. If you're out of here, you've got to come meet my grandma. I'm pretty sure she thinks I'm just making you up as an excuse to visit her less."

I grin at her, shocked by her words and the familiarity we now find ourselves fitting into. But somehow, it just works. Somehow, through this nightmare, I've found a friend.

"I'd love to meet her. I just have to wait for my discharge paperwork."

"Which is right here," a voice calls from the doorway as my nurse appears, waving the papers in the air. "Here we go, here we go." She flips through the stack of papers quickly before handing it to me. "Everything we talked about this morning is in there, including a number to call if you need anything or have any questions." As if she's noticing Jaz for the first time, her eyes land on her. "Oh, hello. What are you doing in here?"

"This is Jaz," I tell her.

"Nice to see you again, Jaz." Nurse Kathy smiles, then looks at me. I hadn't thought about the fact that she likely works this entire hallway, meaning she takes care of Jaz's grandma, too. "Do either of you have any questions?" She points between us. "Is Jaz your ride home, or do we need to call someone?"

"Oh." I hadn't thought of that.

"I'm her ride," Jaz says, nodding with her lips pressed together. Her kindness never fails to shock me.

"Are you sure?" I ask. "It's no big deal to call an Uber."

She wraps her arm around my shoulders, pulling me against her. "I'm your ride, Soph. I told you, you're stuck with me."

Nurse Kathy rests a hand on her hip. "I had no idea the two of you knew each other. What a coincidence."

Before I can answer and tell her we just met, Jaz bumps me with her hip. "Oh, we're besties, Kathy. We go way back." She winks at me, and I can't help but laugh.

"What are the odds," Nurse Kathy says with a whimsical look in her eyes.

My smile grows wide as I look at Jaz, musing over that very sentiment. "We ask ourselves that all the time."

CHAPTER FIVE

5—4:04:29

I avoid touching the food and puzzles all day. I cave and drink water from the tap, but that is it. Even though the chips should be safe in theory, I don't want to chance the fact that any of it could be drugged. I don't want to play into whatever nonconsensual game this is we're currently in the middle of.

But as the day wears on and the hours tick by, my stomach growls, and I feel as much like Simon complaining at his food bowl while waiting for me to feed him as I ever have. By now, Jaz will surely have begun to worry. I have no idea what time it is, but it has begun to get dark outside, and the tiredness of the day has set in.

I pace to the fridge, staring at the meat and cheese waiting there for me, torturing me with their tempting deliciousness.

Why would they need to drug me anyway? They

already have me trapped. What good would it do at this point?

Also, what harm would it do?

The muscles between my legs tense, reminding me of what I suspect has already happened to me, what he's already done, but if I go there, I will spiral, and I can't. I have to be strong. I have to stay focused. I have to think.

In the morning, the man will be back. I close the fridge and return to my small hole in the wall, picking up the spoon with a pit of despair growing in the center of my chest.

I'm not going to be able to do this, but I have to. In the beginning, I kept my thoughts as positive as possible, but now that feels as pointless as everything else. *As pointless as this stupid hole I'm barely digging into this stupid wall. I'm too weak, too slow, too stupid. Stupid enough to have gotten myself into this situation somehow.*

I wish Jaz were here. She'd be able to get me out of this place. If she were with me, I'd never have ended up trapped in the first place. Hence, she's not here.

She's always been the person to cheer me up, to quiet my dark thoughts when I get to a place like this, but for now, I have to do that for myself.

I have to stay positive. If I give up, if I give in to the darkness, he wins. It's as simple as that. *Fake it 'til you make it or whatever, right?*

He will be back with food, and I need to be ready. I know the knife won't work this time, but I could try something else. I could hit him on the head with some-thing heavy if I manage to catch him off guard. I can wait by the door, and then, as soon as he opens it, I'll hit him. Or maybe I'll wait behind the door so I know it's open enough to get a good swing.

It could work.

It could also get me killed.

I throw the spoon down and storm my way back to the fridge. *Fuck it. Who cares if the food is drugged anyway? Death is better than whatever he probably has planned.*

No.

There are worse things than death. If I'm unconscious, I can't fight back.

I shut it again. Where am I going to sleep tonight? In the bed where I woke up? It feels safer there, at least. The couch is unprotected. Anyone could come in and catch me unaware before I'd have time to wake fully.

I'm going to sleep. I'm not going to eat.

I'm going to rest and preserve my energy. Yes, that's what I'll do.

Before I go, though, I open the cabinet and grab an armful of glasses and carry them down the hall to place them inside the doorway. I gather every last dish the kitchen has to offer—plates and bowls—and fill the floor in the entry to the bedroom with them, covering enough space that no human could step over them.

If he tries to come in, he'll either step on the glass dishes and wake me up, or he'll have to try to move them, which will hopefully wake me up and buy me time.

It's not quite genius—Jaz would probably have a better plan—but it is what it is, and it's all I've got. With the bedroom properly barricaded, I sit down on the bed, staring around. I need to remember how I got here. That's what matters most.

I need to remember what happened yesterday. Who brought me here. There was a date, and there was a guy, I'm nearly positive. Someone I met on the dating app.

Maybe.

I can't remember. I can't remember anything.

My brain feels scrambled, my body sore. I hate this, but I will get through it. If I keep saying the words, maybe I'll start to believe it.

I didn't realize I drifted off until I woke up to the sound of shattering glass and a man cursing. I leap off the bed, scrambling to wake the rest of the way up and grab the knife from the nightstand. It won't do much against his armor—likely won't do anything at all—but it's what I have to work with, so it'll have to do.

"Fuck!" the man shouts. "What the hell is this?"

As my vision begins to focus in the dark room, I realize the man isn't wearing his armor this time. Instead, he's dressed in an old Paramore T-shirt and jeans. I know the shirt is old because I was there when we purchased matching ones.

He seems to realize it at the same time I do.

"Sophie?" he asks, his dark brows furrowing as he lurches forward, then back, like he can't decide whether to embrace me or run away. I'm having the same feeling.

"Elliot?" I swallow. I can physically feel my brain trying to put this all together, to make it make sense. "What the hell are you doing here?"

"Why don't you tell me?" he demands. "Where are we?" He stares around, finally stepping over the last of the glass.

I swallow. "Did you bring me here?"

"Did you bring *me* here?" His voice is sharp and accusatory.

"How would I have done that? I woke up here yesterday—this morning—I have no idea what time it is. I have no idea where we are."

He's quiet for a long while, then looks at the ground and back up, one dark brow drawn down. "What do you mean you woke up here?"

"If this is some sort of prank, please just tell me," I say, begging for that to be the case. Begging for this to all be a joke by someone who might be a little bitter over our break-up years ago, but wouldn't actually hurt me.

He shakes his head slowly. "Sophie, I have no idea

what you're talking about. I don't know what the fuck is going on. I haven't seen you in, what, seven years?"

"Seven and a half." I don't know why I admit I know it that well. It's embarrassing, but I will probably always know the exact amount of time that has passed since the day he shattered my heart.

"Right. And now I wake up on a couch in a random-ass apartment I've never been in before in my life. Is this your place? Did we..." He pauses, scratching his stomach. "Did we hook up last night or something? Did we run into each other?"

"I swear to you I don't know." Clearly, he doesn't believe me as I shake my head. "The same thing happened to me. I woke up here." My voice is solemn, riddled with drowsiness and confusion. "I swear it, Elliot. I have no idea what's going on. I'm just as confused as you are."

His eyes dance between mine, trying to understand something that truly can't be understood. "Well, I'm not sticking around," he says with a wave of his hands. "I came in here to see where I was, but I'm out. I don't have time for this."

I follow him as he walks down the hall and to the front door, hoping that he'll be able to escape in some way I couldn't figure out. My chest deflates as I watch him turn the doorknob over and over, trying to comprehend what is happening.

"What the hell?" he mutters under his breath, rubbing sleep from his eyes and stepping back to get a clearer look at the door. His head lifts slowly as he looks it up, then down.

"I'm pretty sure the windows are bulletproof, too," I say. He doesn't turn back to me. "I've tried throwing things into them. Tried picking the lock. I'm digging a hole in the drywall, but it's not going well."

I don't say the next part, the 'we're trapped' part, but I know he understands. When he finally does turn back to me, his eyes look like those of a caged animal. It's the way I felt in those early hours before the panic morphed into determination and surrender, which even now continue to fight for what's left of my resolve.

"We have to keep trying," he says finally, ambling around the room in search of an answer or solution I don't believe, but desperately hope, exists.

I step back as he nods to himself then stalks forward and bends to pick up the oversized coffee table —his strength much more impressive than mine. He launches it forward with a loud, angry groan and huffs as it soars toward the window. I hold my breath, hoping I've been wrong. Hoping I just haven't been strong enough to break through.

When the table rebounds to the floor with a deafening, soul-crushing thud, his shoulders fall. I don't know what to say to him. I never thought I'd see the childhood love of my life again. I certainly never thought we'd be in this situation.

He grabs the table again, throwing it at the window

35

over and over with roars that grow louder each time. I take a seat on the couch, watching with bated breath and hoping for a fate I'm beginning to accept won't come.

That theory is just being further proven the harder he tries. We aren't getting out of here by breaking out, and we have to accept that. Digging through the drywall seems like the best bet—that is if we don't run into concrete—and even that will take several days, working around the clock.

We have to try something else. The sooner he realizes that and accepts it, the better off we'll be.

CHAPTER SIX

BEFORE — THREE YEARS AGO

Something is wrong.

When I walk into Jaz's apartment, the place is a wreck. Half her furniture is missing, including her coffee table and a set of lamps, her curtains and curtain rods, plus a few pictures and most of her record collection, and that's just in the living room.

Her text that asked me to come over earlier didn't hint that anything had happened.

Was she robbed?

Is she okay?

Panic instantly sets in as I shut the door behind me and cross through the living room. "Jaz? Indie?" I search for any sign of my best friend or her roommate while also looking for something I could use as a weapon, should it come to that. "Are you guys here?" When there is still no answer, I picture Jaz and Indie tied up and held hostage. The image of someone else using her phone to send the text and lure me here flashes through my mind. But Jaz is always so smart and careful, not to mention extremely protective of Indie. She wouldn't let that happen.

The sound of something crashing in the bedroom halts my pulse. I freeze, scared to call out again, but not scared enough to bolt. If Jaz is in danger, I have to help her.

Then, before I have the chance to do anything, her bedroom door opens, and she appears. She's wearing an orange crocheted crop top with a green cardigan over it and loose, wide-legged capris.

Her braids are tied back into a low ponytail and her face is stoic when she sees me. She pulls her headphones down to rest around her neck. "Hey. Sorry, I didn't hear you come in."

"Um, I think you were robbed." I gesture around the room.

"Oh." She doesn't bother to look as she makes her way into the kitchen and begins to pour us each a glass of wine. "No, Indie just took all of her stuff. What's left is mine."

My brain sputters to a halt. "Excuse me, what? Why would she do that?" Indie and Jaz have been dating since before I met Jaz. They were best friends. Perfect together. Soulmates. Why would she move out? I can't make it make sense.

Jaz downs the wine in her glass and refills it, then turns to me with a deep inhale. "Because we broke up."

My eyes bug out of my head. "You what? Why? How? When? *Why?*"

"Today."

I don't understand. She's too put together for this incredibly life-altering tragedy. Though Jaz is my friend and Indie is only a friend by default, the idea of losing her is enough to make me cry, so why isn't Jaz? Why doesn't she seem upset?

"Did something happen? Was it a fight? Surely you guys can work it out. You're...you're going to be okay. You have to be okay." Tears fill my eyes as I stare at her, willing her to tell me more than she is.

She looks up toward the light, and for the first time, I catch a hint of the pain in her eyes. Her voice trembles only slightly as she says, "We won't, but I will." She sniffs, drying her eyes and handing over my glass of wine.

"What happened?" I ask, following her into the living room. She plops down on the couch, and I sit next to her. We're long past the point in our friendship where I might've told her she didn't have to talk about it if she didn't want to. Now, I need to know.

"Remember me telling you she wanted to go back to art school?"

I nod.

"Well, she applied all over, thinking she'd probably go

online if it was far away, but she got into a school of design in Rhode Island, one of the really big ones, and it's, like, her dream, so she couldn't pass it up." She shrugs. "And, obviously, I can't go, not with Grandma in the condition she's in. Plus we have the lease here, and it just doesn't make sense to uproot everything and follow her."

I stare at her, still confused. "But couldn't you just date long distance?"

She shrugs one shoulder. "It wouldn't be fair to either of us, you know? Like, sure, we could try it for a month or six months even, but eventually, it would get too hard. Long distance doesn't work. I want her to be able to go and enjoy her time and focus on her stuff without worrying about me."

"I could watch your apartment for you. I could check in on your grandma. You could make this work, I know you can." I don't know why I want to fix this so badly except that I feel like if Jaz and Indie can't make it, what hope is there for the rest of us?

She pats my hand. "I love you for saying that, and I know you would, but I just can't put any of us through that."

"But you love her."

Tears well in her big, chestnut eyes, and her chin quivers as she nods, fighting back sobs. "Yeah, I do. I really, really do." She leans forward then, her head landing on the soft place where my neck meets my shoulder, and I wrap my arms around her, patting her back with my free hand.

I don't know what to say, and I desperately want to say the right thing, but at this moment, I'm not so sure there's a right thing to be said.

She sucks in a ragged, shaky breath, crying silently on my shoulder.

"I'm sorry," I whisper, holding her as close to me as I can. I just want to fix this for her. Jaz is the strongest person I know. When someone this strong breaks in front of you, it's like watching the world flip on its axis. Nothing makes sense.

She pulls back, drying her eyes. "It's done," she says. "We've talked about it over the past few weeks, and we both agreed it's for the best if we just walk away from this as friends rather than dragging it out and letting it die a slow death."

"But—"

She holds up a hand to cut me off. "I love you for trying, but can we please just drink this cheap wine and watch a shitty movie and not pretend like this apartment is currently the tomb of my failed relationship?" She sniffles. "Please?"

I swallow, forcing my lips into a smile. Whatever she needs, I will make it happen. "You're in luck because that's kind of my specialty."

She takes my hand, squeezing it once before she slides back and pulls her legs up in front of her, wrapping her arms around them. I grab the remote in search of something that will make her feel better, smiling to myself over the thought that, in the middle of her life falling apart, I was the one she thought to call.

"You should move in," she says softly. The words catch me off guard, but when I turn back to look at her, her smile is dreamy. She looks like she's falling asleep.

"What?" I ask, turning to face her.

"You hate your roommate." Her eyes open wider, definitely not asleep, as if the thought just occurred to her. "And you don't hate me."

I chuckle. "I definitely don't hate you, but…"

"But nothing. It's the perfect plan. You could have Indie's room." The one she kept as a music room after she and Jaz started dating. "It helps you with your Alexis problem."

My roommate who, I'm convinced, thinks dishes just magically clean themselves.

"And helps me with my lack-of-half-the-rent problem."

I furrow my brows, thinking. "As much as I'd love to be roommates, are you sure? Indie could still change her mind. You guys could get back together, and I don't want to intrude or be the awkward third wheel."

She shrugs one shoulder. "If, in some fairy tale that doesn't exist, that happens, we'll deal with it then. We'll get a bigger apartment." She cocks her head to the side, studying me. "Come on. Have I ever made you feel like a third wheel when we were together?"

"No. Of course not."

"Then move in with me." She sticks out her bottom

lip. "Come on, Soph. I'm *the most* fun. Plus I'm sad right now and only a true monster would want to make me sadder. And also, Alexis is probably home eating your favorite cookies at this exact moment, and I'm vegan, so I'll never eat your favorite cookies!"

"Are you vegan?" I tease. "I hadn't heard."

She shoves my arm, and I slosh wine across the leg of my pants.

"Oh shit!" she cries, putting a hand over her mouth as she giggles. "I'm so sorry."

I jump up and hurry to the kitchen, grabbing a towel to blot out the wet spot. "You're lucky it was white wine."

Still laughing, she says, "That's what you get." Then she adds, "Do you want some pants to change into? I can throw those in the wash."

"Yes, please." I dab up the liquid from my jeans, then start working on the wet spot on the couch.

"Oh." She winces with fake sincerity. "I forgot. Sorry. Laundry's for roomies only."

I blink up at her. "You're the literal worst."

"You love me." She blows me a kiss and stands up, swatting my butt as she jogs into the bedroom and returns moments later with a pair of sweatpants for me to change into.

She dangles them in front of me. "So, what's it going to be? Are we going to be roomies, or are you going to break my heart today, too?"

She's teasing, I know, but we both know it's not

even a question. If Jaz needs me, I'm here. Just like she's always been for me.

"Fine, but Simon's coming, too," I tell her, though I know it won't be an issue. She loves that fat cat more than I do.

"Duh." She tosses the pants at me. "I was just using you to get to him, obvs."

CHAPTER SEVEN

5—3:23:51

When he finally gives up, he staggers backward, red-faced and glistening as he turns to find me. His shirt is painted dark with patches of sweat. Anger washes across his features.

"What the *fuck* is going on?"

I press my lips together. "I told you, I don't know."

"What do you mean you don't know?" He growls, stalking toward me. He takes a seat on the couch next to me, and I breathe in his familiar scent—sweat and soap mixed with the minty cologne he's always worn. I'm surprised, but not disappointed, to find it's still his choice.

Smoothing my hands across my lap, I turn to look at him. Oddly, his panic is only making me calmer. "I mean, I don't know what's going on. I woke up today, this morning, er, maybe yesterday—I don't even know at this point. Regardless, I woke up in a bed I don't recognize. I was hungover, I thought, and I assumed I'd spent the night with someone. But I couldn't find my phone or my purse. I came out of the bedroom, looking for the person I apparently spent the night with, but no one was here. When I realized I was locked in, I tried to pick the lock with everything I could find, tried to break through the windows, but nothing worked. I was trapped." I look down, studying my fingers. When I look back up at him, his expression is filled with concern, and I so badly want to tell him it'll all be okay, but the truth is I have no idea if it will be. I can lie to myself, but I can't lie to him. "So then, I noticed this." I gesture behind me to the countdown on the wall.

"What is i—"

Before he can finish his question, the last number changes, giving him an answer.

"A countdown?"

I nod.

"To what?"

"I have no idea. There is a man who comes and—"

"A man?" he shouts, standing up. "You've seen someone else here?"

I put a hand up, quieting him. "If you'll let me finish." I pause, proving my point. "There's a man who comes to bring us food. At least, he brought me one meal and promised another tomorrow. He dresses in this sort of nylon, ninja-looking material. I tried to stab him, but—"

He balks. "Excuse me, what? You tried to *stab* him? What the fuck, Sophie?"

"It's fine. It didn't work anyway. My knife wouldn't go through the material. But I was scared and alone and trapped, and I didn't know what to do except attack and hope for the best. I thought I was doing the right thing."

"What did he do? After...after you tried to stab him, I mean." His eyes flash with something dark that doesn't deserve to be there. A jealousy that I once thrived off of. "Did he hurt you?"

I shake my head. "No. He was...oddly calm. He said that I know why I'm here and that I'm safe, or something along those lines. I don't know. My head is such a mess. I'm pretty sure I was drugged or something. I didn't drink enough to black out." I have no idea if it's true, but the longer we're here, the more sure I am that it is. "What's the last thing you remember?"

He rests his head in his hands. "I was..." There's a long, drawn-out pause before he lifts his head again, looking at me. "I don't know. I was on a date, I think, but it's like..." He waves a hand around his head like a cloud of smoke is billowing out of it, and it's the perfect representation of how I feel. "I can't remember." His eyes widen. "Were we both drugged?"

"Do you have your phone?" I ask, knowing the answer before he gives it.

His head shakes slowly as he pats his pockets. "I couldn't find it when I woke up. I just assumed I'd left it in whoever's bedroom. I never thought…" His eyes find mine again, and if these circumstances were different, I might say it's really good to see him. "I never thought I'd see you again."

"Well." I push a breath of air out of my nose. "We live in the same town. I think it was inevitable at some point. Why not when we've both been kidnapped?"

He gives me a look that says I should be serious, but we both know humor is my favorite coping mechanism. My second favorite—alcohol—doesn't seem to exist in this box of an apartment.

"So what are we going to do?" he asks, searching around the room with his eyes. "There has to be a way out. Something you haven't tried."

"I keep thinking so too, but I don't know where it would be. The door and windows won't work. I've tried shouting, but if there are neighbors nearby, they definitely don't care to help. As far as I can tell, the only way out is to ambush the guy when he brings us dinner again. Now that there are two of us—"

He lets out something that sounds like a scoff. "I just don't understand. It doesn't make sense. How would they have found us? Why would they have made this connection? I haven't spoken to you in years. We aren't even Facebook friends anymore. How would they have known we had a history? Why would they have brought us here?"

"I don't know," I say simply. I refuse to admit that I don't want to question it too hard because I'm afraid

I'll have to wake up from this dream. Even if he broke my heart years ago, even if I'd rather it be anyone else here with me, I'm grateful to see a familiar face and have someone to talk to.

Aaand that makes me an asshole. Cool.

"Are you seeing anyone?"

I open my mouth to answer, but stop, confused and surprised by the question.

He rushes to explain, swiping a hand across the back of his neck like he does when he's put under pressure. "I'm just—I'm wondering if you mentioned me to someone. That we'd dated in the past. Not because I care or anything, but because, well, who else would know?"

"No, I get it. But I'm not seeing anyone. Not seriously anyway. I've probably mentioned you to a few people over the last almost-decade, yeah, but who would've known how to find you? It has to be related to something from back then, right?"

"You mean like that secret murder we committed years ago and now someone is back to exact revenge?" He gives a dry laugh. "This isn't one of those cheesy thriller novels you read, Soph."

"They're not cheesy, and I'm serious. There's no way this is a coincidence. For it to be both of us? How could it be?"

He stands, running his hands through his dark locks. "No, I know you're right. I just—"

Before he can say anything, there's the familiar

sound of whistling outside the door. It's a tune I don't recognize, but I know it's him. We haven't prepared for this. We don't have weapons. Knives won't work. The blender, maybe? To hit him over the head?

Elliot's eyes search mine before he darts across the room to the door, ready to stop the man from coming inside. When the door cracks open, Elliot is there, standing in front of him. He lodges his foot in the opening to keep the man from closing it while he has one hand on the frame and the other on the door itself to keep it from opening farther.

"Who are you?" he barks. "Let us out of here." He struggles against the door, trying to keep it open while the man tries desperately to pull it shut with one hand. Then Elliot freezes and retreats, his entire body stiff as a board.

"Back up." Hands in the air, Elliot does as he's told, and when the man comes into view this time, I see he has a gun in his hands. It's as if I've suddenly been doused with ice water, every muscle in my body ice cold. Aside from a few shotguns my dad kept around the house for hunting, I've never seen a gun in person, and certainly not one pointed at me. I should've known he wouldn't come unarmed this time after what I tried to do before. "No one do anything stupid, and I won't have to use this."

I nod, my hands up, too, as Elliot comes to stand next to me, both of our backs against the wall as the man places a new box on the counter and unpacks it with his free hand. This time there are two platters of food. They were prepared for both of us to be here. Realistically, I knew they would be, but somehow, it just makes this all feel more premeditated and terrifying.

"Do you have any trash you want me to take?" the man asks, his voice almost charming, like he's a waiter and not the monster holding us captive against our will.

I shake my head.

"What do you want from us, man?" Elliot asks. "Why are you doing this?"

The man doesn't answer, just puts the lid back on the box and backs away from us. "I'll be back tomorrow," he says before he slips out the door. A promise and a warning.

When I hear the lock click, tears prick my eyes.

CHAPTER EIGHT

BEFORE — TWO YEARS AGO

"Happy birthday to you!" Jaz cheers as the waiter sets the small cake between us. Before he can walk away, she asks, "This is vegan, right?"

"Yes, ma'am," he says, waving a hand at the cake. "We made sure."

She claps her hands as the single candle sparks, waiting for me to blow it out. I glare at her as I do it, making my best effort to appear entirely unimpressed. She promised me she wasn't going to make a big fuss out of my birthday, but I knew it was a lie. Especially when the entire day had gone by without a phone call or text from my parents.

She giggles and dips her finger in the icing, then plops it on my nose. I roll my eyes at her, grabbing a napkin to wipe away the mess as she places a fork in front of me before she digs into her side of the cake.

"What did you wish for?" she asks, licking a bit of icing from her upper lip.

I wad the napkin up and set it down, taking my first bite as I think. "I forgot to make a wish."

Her eyes go wide, jaw slack, and she slaps her hand on the table. "Excuse me? You *forgot* to make a wish?"

I squeeze my eyes shut, remaining silent as I count to three. "There, happy? I made a wish."

"You can't do it after the fact!" she cries. "Don't you know how birthday wishes go?"

"Well, I'm not twelve, so no."

"Oooh." She takes another bite, wagging her fork at me. "Have I taught you nothing with my years and years of wisdom?"

"You've taught me plenty. I just must've missed class the day we discussed birthday wishes."

She digs into her purse and pulls out a lighter.

"Grandma wouldn't approve of you smoking," I tease.

She purses her lips. We both know the lighter is for sage, which she seems to carry with her everywhere, always looking for an opportunity to clear away bad energy. She lifts the lighter to the candle's wick and relights it. "Now, blow. And this time, make a wish."

I close my eyes, thinking. It's fine. It's stupid, really. I'm just not into all this wish nonsense like Jaz is. Fate and energy and crystals and magic. She's like a walking poster child for everything spiritual and otherworldly. She doesn't just talk about it to be cool or trendy or whatever, she truly, genuinely believes in it. I, on the other hand, do not. But, for Jaz, I'll play along.

I lean forward, closing my eyes and trying to think of what to wish for. I'm happy for the first time in so long. I have a friend. A true friend who cares about me and checks on me and listens to me. Someone I don't have to walk on eggshells around. I have a job I don't totally hate. I have an apartment in a safe neighborhood, with a roommate who doesn't steal my food. I don't know what else I could want, except…

I want to know where my life is going.

I want direction.

I want to finally have a path to walk down, to know what my life will look like in ten years, because the bitter reality is I can't work at the coffee shop forever. And eventually, Jaz is going to find someone to date seriously, and they're going to build a life together.

That thought hits me down deep in my chest, sending a pang of sadness through me. I wish things could stay exactly like they are, but short of that, and knowing that's illogical, *I wish I could always be this happy.*

With that thought ringing in my head, I blow out the candle, and Jaz cheers again.

"What did you wish for?" she asks when I open my eyes.

"If I tell you, it won't come true." I take another bite of the cake, and she eyes me, jabbing her fork playfully in my direction.

"But I can make all your wishes come true," she teases, waving her hands through the air.

"Fine. I wished for the last bite of cake." I take the final bite with a wry grin. "And to go home and go to bed." I stand up, grab my purse, and reach for her hand. "Holy shit, look at that. You really are magic."

She cackles as I tug her up from her seat, leaning over the table to down the last of her wine and grab our receipt before we go.

Outside the restaurant, while we wait for the valet to get her car, she sways in place to the sound of "Hey There, Delilah" being played by a musician down the street. "I love this song."

"Me too," I admit. "I haven't heard it in ages."

When the car arrives, she tips the valet, and we sink into our seats. She shimmies her shoulders at me. "So where to next, birthday girl?"

"I told you, home and bed."

"You want to stop by Grandma's first?" she teases. "*She's* probably still awake."

"Don't tempt me with a good time. You know I will visit Grandma any day."

The chuckle that escapes her lips is soft. "She loves you."

I stifle a yawn as I lean my head back on the seat, staring out the window at the city lights as they pass by. As a kid, one of my favorite things was driving through the city at night, seeing all the lights lit up like stars.

It always made everything feel a little bit magical.

"Hey," she says, pausing the music.

I turn my head to look at her.

"Ever since everything that happened with *Smelliot*—"

I snort at the nickname she's given my ex.

"Why haven't you dated anyone else?"

Something heavy settles in my chest. "I don't know," I admit. I'd be lying if I said I didn't think about it sometimes, but the truth is that it scares me more now than it ever did before. And maybe it scares me most of all because there was never an argument or huge fight that ended things for Elliot and me. He just slipped away like I was easy to forget. I'm scared to let someone in again, to trust someone, to give them that power over me. It feels like the most vulnerable thing in the world. But I don't want to say any of that, though I suspect Jaz knows it all. This is supposed to be a happy night, and happiness is where I'm choosing to focus. "I guess it just never really felt worth it. I'm happy."

She nods, twisting her hands on the steering wheel.

"Why?"

"No reason. Just trying to keep you awake." She sticks her tongue out at me, and I scowl.

"I'm not falling asleep."

"You were snoring."

"Whatever," I quip. "Leave me alone. It's my birthday." I turn in my seat so I'm facing the window, then look back over my shoulder. "Anyway, what about you? You and Indie broke up years ago now. I don't see you back out there."

"I was finding myself." Her voice takes on a grand resonance.

"And did you like what you found?" I turn back to face her.

"I did, actually. Turns out, I'm pretty fabulous."

I yawn again. "I'm inclined to agree."

She presses play on the music, and I lay my head back on the seat again, closing my eyes. "Thank you for tonight, by the way. You were right, that place was amazing."

"I don't eat at bad places, Soph. When will you learn that?"

"When you stop taking me to bad places," I retort.

"Name one." She pauses the music again as we pull into our neighborhood.

"That Italian restaurant with the burned bread and crunchy lasagna."

Her jaw drops. "You picked that place."

"You let me."

Pinching her lips together, she eyes me. "I tried to warn you about that restaurant, if I remember correctly. I didn't like the look of it. It was too clean."

"Too clean?" I scoff, sitting up further in my seat as we pull into the parking lot. "How is that a thing?"

"The best places have a little bit of a vibe to 'em, you know? It shouldn't look like a hospital. There weren't

57

crumbs anywhere to be seen. Nothing sticky on the floor." She shrugs, curling her upper lip with disgust. "I didn't trust it."

Unbuckling as I roll my eyes, I wait for her to stop the car before stepping out and leading the way toward our building. "Well, for your birthday, I'll be sure to take you to the dumpster behind a Denny's. Some would call that a vibe."

She throws her head back with a belly laugh. "You tease, but that wouldn't be much better than the place you took me last year."

"It was a vegan restaurant!" I say.

"An *empty* vegan restaurant." She clicks her tongue and pushes the door to the apartment open. "See, this is what I'm talking about. There are *signs*. You don't pay enough attention, Soph."

She does say that a lot, and to be fair, she's not wrong. "Are we fighting right now?"

A hand goes to her chest like she's offended. "What kind of friend would I be if I fought with the birthday girl?" At the sound of our voices, Simon comes darting into the room. She bends down and lifts him from the ground, rubbing her face against his side. "I wouldn't do that, would I, Sci-Fi?"

Like the little betraying asshole he is, Simon purrs against her in an instant. I cross my arms. "Traitor."

She places him down, tugging me into a hug. "You know I'm teasing. The vegan place was nice."

"You hated it," I say, my voice low and monotone, face tucked against her chest.

"But I loved being there with you, and that's all that matters." She pulls back and places a kiss on the top of my head, then saunters down the hall toward her bedroom. In the kitchen, I refill Simon's food and make myself a glass of water.

Before I turn out the light to head for bed, Jaz's bedroom door opens, and she returns in her pajamas, face freshly washed. "What do you say? *Grace and Frankie* marathon for old times?" It's become our thing, not only a huge part of what brought us closer during those early days in the hospital, but a picture of our lives together. She is clearly Frankie, which I suppose makes me Grace, though I'm not sure I fit that mold either.

"Sounds perfect."

She holds out her hand for me, and I slip my palm into hers as we disappear into my bedroom. She flops on the bed while I change into my pajamas, wash my face, and brush my teeth. When I return, she's already under the covers with the show ready to start.

I flip off the lamp and slide under the covers next to her, already dozing off when she pushes play.

After a few moments, I feel her running her hands through my hair, twisting the locks into braids. "Do you want me to turn it off?" she whispers.

"No. I'm awake," I lie, rubbing my eyes and adjusting in bed. I'm starting to doze off again when she turns off the TV and slips out of bed, but I stop her, reaching out my hand and grasping her arm. "Stay," I whine. "Birthday wish."

"You're not supposed to tell me your wish." She hesitates, but eventually, I feel her slip back into bed behind me. The heat radiating off her body warms me to my core, and I roll over to face her, smiling to myself.

"Good night."

"Good night," she whispers, her voice soft and cracking. I can't tell if it's from sleep or if something is bothering her, so I flick the lamp back on.

"Is everything okay?"

She nods, but her eyes are distant.

"Jaz." I trail my finger over her arm. "What's wrong? Are you mad I fell asleep?"

She purses her lips. "Of course not."

"You seem upset."

Blinking, she stares at me, opening her mouth like she wants to say something, then closing it again. "What did you really wish for tonight?"

I smile, but somehow it feels sad. "I wished to always be this happy."

She swallows, eyes dipping down to land on my lips. "Are you happy?"

"Duh." My heart is racing as my hand slows on her arm until it's resting just above her elbow. "Are you?"

She nods, her lips parting, and when her eyes meet mine, there's something molten behind them. Her hand comes up to cup my face, and she brushes hair from my eyes with her thumb. I know what's coming, but I'm also sure it's impossible. I'm sure it's just a dream.

"Jaz…"

"Just…" She doesn't finish that thought. Instead, her mouth comes down on mine, soft and pillowy and absolutely perfect. She kisses me slowly at first, tentatively. This is a line we've never crossed, not that I haven't thought about it. She's been my friend, my best friend, but there is nothing friendly about this kiss. Soft kisses turn to demanding ones as she pulls me into her. My hands skim over her shirt, over her breasts, and I can't believe this is happening. I want everything all at once, yet I also want this to move at a snail's pace. I want to savor every moment. I want to never wake up from this dream.

"Is this okay?" She pulls back, eyeing me with a look of worry.

I kiss her in answer, hoping it's a balm to ease any fear she might have. "Nothing has ever been this okay," I promise her, only letting our lips part for the time it takes to utter those words. Her lips find mine again, our kisses beautiful juxtapositions. Fierce and tender, passionate and timid, eager and reluctant.

She sighs against my mouth, running her nails up my back, and I've never experienced a more perfect moment in my life. I didn't know my heart could beat so fast.

New birthday wish: Please let it always be like this. Please let me keep her.

CHAPTER NINE

5—3:23:17

Elliot turns back to look at me, his eyes wide. "Are you okay?"

I nod slowly, running my hands over myself. "I'm fine." We both know it's a lie. How could either of us be fine?

He runs his tongue over his bottom lip, staring up at the ceiling, then across the room. "Did you recognize his voice?"

"No, I don't think so. Did you?" It's possible—incredibly likely, in fact—that this person is someone we both know.

Chewing his lip, he shakes his head. "No. I don't think so either. Maybe they're using some sort of voice changer."

"Wouldn't that make them sound robotic?"

"I have no idea. I'm sure there's some sort of technology out there that could make them sound like anything they want." After rubbing his hand down his face with a sigh, he approaches the countertop that separates the kitchen and living room to check out the food. "I'm starving. Have you been eating what he brings you?"

"No." I'm proud of myself for the willpower I've shown, but I'm not sure how much longer I can hold out. I just want to eat. My stomach feels as if it's collapsing in on itself. Imagine that—we're probably about to be killed, if not worse, and all I can think about is food.

Without touching the food, he leans down and sniffs it carefully. I watch him, holding my breath.

"It smells okay, but if it's drugged or poisoned, I'm not sure that it would smell."

"Maybe one of us should eat it," I suggest, looking pointedly at him.

One corner of his mouth quirks. "And I suppose that should be me?"

I don't respond. It's not like I want Elliot to die, obviously. I just…also don't want to die myself. And he's older, though only by a year, so he's lived longer. It's only fair, really.

"You'd like that, wouldn't you?" he teases, but there's a bit of hurt in his voice I don't miss.

"You getting food poisoning when we don't have a change of clothes or a way to wash laundry? It's not exactly on my bucket list, no."

He chuckles. "Fair enough." Then his eyes go serious. "How long has it been since you've eaten?"

"Um…" I look toward the countdown clock, though I can't see it from where we're standing. "I don't know, honestly. A day and a half?"

"Okay." His face goes serious as he stares at the food. "We have to try this. You can't go much longer without food, and we don't know how much longer we'll be in here."

"We can wait," I promise him. "At least a few more days. People can survive weeks without eating."

He studies the food a moment longer, lifting a piece of cheese off of the platter, but eventually puts it down. "If you're sure."

I stifle a yawn, jutting my chin toward the kitchen. "We should put it in the fridge with the other one, just in case. But maybe we could try the chips. Something to hold us over. I mean, they're packaged and sealed. How bad could they be?" I eye the bag of plain potato chips, and my first thought is of Jaz and how she'd be thrilled that they're vegan, even if nothing else we've been brought is.

I miss my best friend so much it hurts. I wish I could tell her about everything that's going on. Even if I couldn't get out of here, I wish I could talk to her.

He does as I've suggested, then shuts the fridge and opens the bag of chips, taking one, sniffing it, then popping it into his mouth. "I know this is probably a weird thing to say right now, but I'm glad to see you."

The words land somewhere in my sternum, twisting with meaning and surprise. "You are?"

He takes a step toward me, looking down like he's suddenly embarrassed. "Well, better you than a stranger, I guess."

A dry chuckle escapes my throat without warning. "Wow. Thanks."

He brushes my shoulder as he walks past me, dropping his chin low with a yawn of his own. "I don't feel great," he admits, holding his stomach.

"Oh, god. The chips?"

The bag in his hand suddenly feels like a red warning signal, a huge 'only idiots would eat this' sign. His brows draw together as he looks at the bag. "Sorry, no. I mean that I feel hungover."

"Yeah, I think that's from whatever they've given us to get us here. I woke up yesterday feeling sick."

He drops onto the couch in the living room, stretching out and eating a few more chips before holding the bag out to me. "We have a day until he's back, right?"

Slowly, I cross the room, watching him carefully for any signs that he is starting to feel off. I don't know how quickly these things work, but the scent of the salt in the air is making my mouth water. "That's what he said."

"I'm going to rest, then." He opens one eye to look at me. "Not because I'm suddenly tired from being drugged by these chips, but because we need rest. You should get some sleep, too."

I scoff, finally taking a single chip out of the bag and popping it into my mouth. "We've been kidnapped. Don't you think we should come up with a plan?" I seal the bag up, refusing to eat any more until I see how this makes me feel, but I'll take the bag to my bedroom for safe keeping.

"I just told you the plan. We rest for a few hours, then decide how we're going to escape when he comes here next time."

"You're seriously just going to sleep?" I cross my arms and stare at him in disbelief.

He's quiet for a moment, then props up on one arm, grinning at me. "Unless you want to reminisce about old times or profess your undying love for me."

I turn away from him abruptly. "I'd rather be kidnapped."

In the bathroom, I wash my face in the sink and scrub my hair with my head over the bathtub with hand soap since it's all we've been given. It doesn't matter in the grand scheme of things, I know, but something about getting clean again makes me feel like things aren't so bad.

I open several empty drawers, nearly giving up when I find one that contains two unopened tooth-brushes and a tube of toothpaste. I could practically cry.

I rip the protective seal off the toothpaste and tear

open my toothbrush, brushing my teeth like a madwoman for a ridiculous amount of time. I'm taking so long that dentists would probably have an issue with it, but I don't care.

With minty-fresh breath, I stick my head out the door and call to him, "There's toothpaste and a new toothbrush in here for you if you need it."

Without waiting to hear his response, I make my way into the bedroom and shut the door. I can't help wondering if the toothbrushes were always there, a clue right under my nose that he would be coming, and I just missed it. Or if someone brought the toothpaste and toothbrushes last night when they brought Elliot in.

I also wonder how I didn't manage to wake up when they did that. There are two doors to the bathroom, one from the bedroom and one from the hallway. I had both entrances into the bedroom—the one from the en suite and the one from the hallway—covered with dishes that would wake me if someone tried to enter the room, but I never thought to cover the bathroom doorway from the hallway, just in case someone were to try and get inside the bathroom. I was only concerned with someone trying to enter the bedroom.

Now, I'm wondering if I should be guarding every single door with dishes. I cleaned them all up earlier, placing the unbroken dishes back in the cabinets, but maybe that was a mistake. I've always been a deep sleeper, but the thought scares me now more than ever. What else might I sleep through?

Soon, I hear the water running in the bathroom and smile to myself as I hear Elliot brushing his teeth. It all feels normal and safe as I close my eyes, pretending that it is, even if just for a moment.

I spend the first hour in bed tossing and turning, replaying everything that has happened today and wondering what will happen next. Elliot wasn't wrong when he said being together again is better than being alone, but not by much.

I'm glad to have someone else here, should the worst thing happen, but Elliot broke my heart when he left me. I thought we'd be together forever. I thought he was the one, so when he dumped me out of nowhere with no real explanation, it left me devastated.

If I was ever going to see him again, I hoped it would be when I was looking my best, at the top of my game. Definitely not like this—with unbrushed hair, no deodorant, and dirty, wrinkled clothing—not in a situation where I'm terrified.

Still, I'm glad he's here, even if I can't make sense of why he is.

The sun is shining brilliantly through the curtains next to me when I open my eyes, and the apartment is silent. *He's still sleeping.*

After a few minutes of lying in total silence with my thoughts while I wake the rest of the way up, I get out of bed and slip into the bathroom, where I take a full, quick shower to rinse my body. I open the drawer and notice his toothbrush is missing. *Seriously? Did he think I was going to, like, scrub the toilet with it or something?*

Oh my god, did he scrub the toilet with mine?

Cautiously, I lift my toothbrush to my nose, feeling like an idiot, and sniff. I smell only toothpaste, thankfully. After brushing my teeth again and rinsing my mouth with a handful of water, I feel better—cleaner anyway—though I still have to slip into my old clothes, and I know I'll instantly feel gross again. It's better than nothing, I guess.

After cleaning up and getting dressed, I head into the living room, wondering why he still isn't awake. It's funny. I used to know so much about him—everything, I thought—but for the life of me, I can't remember if he's an early riser or if he preferred to sleep in. I guess now I have my answer.

Or not.

In the living room, I pause when I realize the couch is empty. There's not even an outline in the fabric of the place where he slept. The kitchen is silent, too.

"Elliot?" I call, searching around. "Where are you?"

There's no reply. I walk around the living room as if I'm expecting him to jump out and try to scare me, cautiously checking behind curtains and next to the couch. In the kitchen, I look in the small pantry and in the closet in the bedroom.

I check the bathroom again, already knowing he can't be there.

But if he's not there…he's nowhere. The realization slams into my chest as I run across the apartment and turn the doorknob, hoping with all the hope left inside me that he found a way to escape and left it open for me, but it isn't. It's as locked as it's ever been.

The apartment is completely empty. I spin in place, my head throbbing.

I'm all alone. Was it all a dream before? Did I imagine everything?

CHAPTER TEN

BEFORE — ONE YEAR AND SIX MONTHS AGO

"We need to talk."

The words are a gut punch before I can even turn around and see her face. When I do, Jaz stands in the doorway to my bedroom, her expression unreadable. I drop the shirt I'd been folding on the bed, taking in the sight of her.

"Is everything okay?" I hold out my hands to her, but she doesn't take them.

She walks into the room, leaning on the desk against the wall. "Brynne and Curtis broke up."

The words wash over me, bringing first sadness, then relief. "Oh. Oh, that's awful." I want to say something much less considerate, like, *Is that all?* but I can't bring myself to do it.

"She needs our help getting her stuff out of his place this weekend."

I nod slowly. "Okay, sure. She's letting him keep the

apartment? Does she need a place to stay?" Over the past six months, Jaz and I have taken things slow. We haven't exactly put a label on things, though we've acted as much like a couple as any relationship I've ever been in. There's no reason I couldn't move into her room like Indie did for a while, so Brynne has a place to crash.

"No." She folds her arms across her chest, still not quite looking at me. "She's moving back in with her sister for a few months until she gets back on her feet."

"Okay." I wait for whatever else is obviously on her mind. "Poor Brynne. Is she okay? Should we go over and take her out for the night?"

"She said she's okay. Curtis went to stay with a friend so she can pack everything."

"Are you okay?" I ask flat out. I've been trying to get better about asking what I actually want to know rather than beating around the bush, though it definitely doesn't come naturally to me.

She sucks in a deep breath, then meets my eyes finally. When she does, her eyes are filled with tears.

Without thinking, I launch forward, grasping her arms. "What's wrong? You're scaring me."

She shakes me off, beginning to pace. "I love you, Soph."

The laugh that escapes me sounds robotic and terrified. "I love you too." I don't know if we're saying it as friends or something more, but either way, it's true.

"You're my best friend."

A balloon in my chest pops all at once, deflating in an instant. *I'm losing her, and I never really had her.* I wait in silence for the bomb to drop.

"I don't want to lose you."

"What do you mean?" I ask, hating how whiny my voice sounds. "What happened?"

"Nothing," she says quickly. "Nothing. I just, look, I've been thinking. Panicking, really."

"About?"

"About Curtis and Brynne." She hesitates. "And Indie and me."

It feels as if I've been slammed into a brick wall as I take a step back, sinking onto the bed. "Oh."

"When she moved in here, we were best friends, too. And then, and then we broke up, and now we haven't spoken in years. And Curtis and Brynne, same thing. They'd been friends forever before they started dating, and now it's all gone."

"What are you talking about?" My vision blurs with betraying tears as I stare at her, the red of her overalls transforming into a watercolor painting.

"I just"—she swipes her hand over her mouth—"I don't want to, *no*, I *refuse* to lose you. And I know this is totally unfair, and I know I'm the one who made the first move, but Soph, you're my best friend. You mean so much to me, and I just can't do it. I can't risk this. Us. You. I can't lose you."

"You're not going to lose me," I tell her, standing up and taking a step toward her. "I promise you won't."

She holds up a hand to stop me from coming any closer. "You say that now, and I know you mean it, and I want to believe it more than I've ever wanted anything, but I have to be realistic. It's breaking my heart to do this." Her hand goes to her chest like she can feel the pain I'm feeling too, but if she could, there's no way she would be able to go through with it. "Because I do love you, in every way that matters. I want to think this can work, that we can make this work—"

"But you're not willing to try. I'm not worth the risk."

It's her turn to walk toward me, holding my arms in her hands. "You're worth every risk, which is why I'm doing this. Because if I have to break my heart to keep you, I will." She cocks her head to the side, and even with tears streaming down her face, she's the most beautiful person I've ever seen in my life. "Please tell me you understand. Tell me you don't hate me." Her voice cracks as she says the last sentence, and I feel it deep inside myself. I feel her pain, as real as my own, but hers is the one I have to fix first.

Even if I don't agree, I understand why she's doing this. We've both been burned by people we thought we could trust, lost friendships and pieces of ourselves over it. Our friendship is too important to lose.

If I lost her, I'd lose everything.

"I don't hate you." I throw my arms around her,

hugging her tightly to keep her from seeing how broken I am. "I could never hate you."

As she pulls away, there's a moment when she almost kisses me. I see it in her eyes, how close she is to doing it. How easy it would be to slip back into old habits and pretend this conversation never happened. But then, she just...doesn't. She drops her arms away from me and steps back farther, bowing her head and dusting her fingers under her eyes.

"I'm sorry," she whispers. "I wish..."

"I know." She doesn't need to say any more. "I wish, too."

Without another word, she backs out into the hallway, closing the door to my room as quickly as she closed the door to our relationship. Just like that, it's as if it never happened.

It's better this way, really. At least that's what I'll tell myself until I start to believe it. I turn back to the laundry I was folding, trying not to let her hear me cry. Trying not to hear the sounds of her own crying in the next room.

We're broken right now, but this can be fixed.

We both know there are things that just can't be, and this is the smartest, safest way to move forward. Protecting our friendship is the most important thing.

Stupid Soph, you should've known wishes don't come true.

CHAPTER ELEVEN

5—3:17:41

I search the apartment again, high and low, repeating my steps until I know the layout of the place with my eyes closed. I check the bathroom and the closets and the pantry. I check behind curtains and under cushions, like he might be playing some weird game of hide-and-seek. I call for him, and the action feels eerily reminiscent of the days I spent curled up in bed, sobbing his name.

I look for a sign that he was even here, that any of it happened at all, but it's not there. Starting with the missing toothbrush, which I thought nothing of earlier, and ending with the fact that when I check the fridge, there is only one platter of food.

It was a dream.

That realization is probably the hardest of them all, which makes no sense. I should care more that I've been kidnapped, but the pain of being alone again—of never having *not* been alone—is worse.

It was all a dream. Some weird, sleep- and food-deprived dream, and I don't understand why my mind would go to him specifically. Why would he be who I thought of? And why do I miss him so badly now?

It's like those moments when you wake up from a dream about someone you've never thought romantically of in your life and your brain can't differentiate between what's real and what definitely is not.

I so desperately want it to have been real. I want to think he's been here. I want to not be alone. I want to be with someone who cares—*cared*.

I'm melting, I think. The walls of my resolve are finally crumbling. I thought I had it together. I thought I was getting through this. Problem solving and sorting through my issues and figuring out a way to escape this place, but apparently not. Apparently I've held it together absolutely as long as my brain will allow, and now this is it.

I make my way into the living room, dropping face down onto the couch. My nose brushes the fabric, and I wait for a hint of him, a whiff of his familiar cologne, but it's not there.

He's not here. He was never here.

Tears spill out of my eyes, and I just want to go back to sleep. I just want to go back to the place where I was safe and not alone, even if it's not real. I don't want to be here anymore.

Not here in this room, not here in this headspace.

I glance up at the countdown clock on the wall, which reads:

5—3:17:41

Whatever is going to happen in three days, I need to be ready, but at this moment, I can't bring myself to care.

I need food. I need water.

I've been here before, depressed and wallowing, and I can't do it again. I can't allow myself to go there because I know what will happen if I do. I know if I let myself sink, I will sink and sink and sink until I drown. Therapy has gotten me to a place where I'm better. Healthier. I have the strength to cope.

I can do this.

I will do this.

I stand from the couch and walk toward the sink, where I make a glass of water and down it quickly, then I do ten jumping jacks to get my heart pumping.

Next, it's time for the fridge. I don't have a choice. If I want to survive, if I want to keep my strength up, I have to try it. I pick up a slice of cheese and take a nibble, then wait.

When my stomach doesn't hurt, and the food doesn't taste off, I pop the rest of the cheese slice into my mouth and reach for a piece of meat. I eat it too and then force myself to close the fridge. Like last night with the chips, I'm hoping I've eaten enough that it will prove if the food is poisoned without the chance of actually killing me.

I refill my glass of water and carry it with me to the couch, where I tuck my legs up underneath me and stare at nothing at all, very aware of my head and my stomach and how they both feel. Every twinge in my gut is a warning of impending doom. Every spot in my vision is a confirmation that I've surely hurt myself. That this stupid decision will be my last.

I have no willpower, or not as much as I thought I had anyway.

Jaz would call me an idiot if she were here. She'd have made it longer without eating. Hell, she'd probably already be out of here if she were in this position. Actually, scratch that, she'd never have allowed herself to get into this position in the first place.

She's too smart. She had involved parents who cared and older sisters who taught her these things. She's the one who installed extra locks on our door. She's the one who taught me to check the backseat before getting into the car. She bought me those scrunchies that cover our drinks when we're out in public. She's not going to slip up even once. She'd never be in this position.

I can't stop thinking about her and what she must be thinking by now. Without a doubt, she's noticed I'm not there and will have tried to call my phone a thousand times. Will whoever has my phone have texted her and tried to pretend I'm still with my date? Will she believe it?

Maybe. Probably. For a day or two. But after that... she'll start to worry. She'll check in with Margie at The Bold Bean, but then what? Will she call my parents? Doubtful since we haven't spoken more than once or twice a year since I graduated from high school. What about the police? If I know Jaz, I think that'll be a last resort. Not only because she doesn't totally trust them, but because she won't want to make a scene over nothing if it turns out that I'm fine. That I just didn't need her.

Which means we'll be cutting it down to the wire for her to realize something's wrong, make the decision to report it, and have the police looking for me before my countdown runs out.

What then?

I think of my parents and wonder when she'll make the decision to tell them or if she will at all. We aren't estranged, necessarily. Nothing has happened to make me cut them off. There just came a point when, through therapy, I realized our relationship was never going to be what I hoped for. My parents will never be the type of parents to think about me or check up on me. I will always have to call or text them first. They will always put their own needs and the needs of my brother and his kids before me, and because I no longer live in our small town, I will always be an afterthought. It's a hard thing to accept. Painful and stressful and filled with moments of relapsing—of considering throwing everything I've built and worked for away to go back and earn their acceptance, but it would never be enough. I'm only enough if I'm living my life in the way they want, and that would never be okay with me in the long run. It would mean a life of resentment and a constant cycle of trying to earn their approval over and over again.

When choosing between my own happiness and the approval of someone else—even if it's my parents—I've finally learned that I have to choose my own happiness. Even when it stings. Even when it hurts so badly I feel as if I'm shredding my own skin. Even when I feel utterly alone and misunderstood.

Someday, I hope, I will be glad I've done it.

So, no. I don't think Jaz will call them anytime soon, but part of me wants her to. Would they come to the city to help in the search? My parents aren't heartless. I know they'll worry. I know they'll be devastated if anything happens to me. Part of me thinks it wouldn't be the worst thing if they worried for just a day or so.

I place my glass on the coffee table and grab a puzzle box from the delivery on my first day here out of the drawer in the coffee table, dumping the pieces out. I still feel fine physically, which is a good thing, but I need to keep my mind busy and active until my next meal is brought to me, by which time, I'll be ready to escape.

CHAPTER TWELVE

BEFORE — TWO WEEKS AGO

Jaz leans across the couch, snatching a handful of potato chips from the bag between my legs. She eyes my phone screen with a look of disgust. "Why the hell does every man think their dating profile photo should be them with a fish they've caught? Who is impressed by that?"

I snort. "Apparently someone."

"Literally no one. Someone should tell them." She rolls her eyes. "It's disgusting. And don't get me started on the ones who post pictures with bloody deer carcasses. Like, hello, some of us aren't animal killers, you know?"

"Well, it's a good way to know who *not* to talk to then."

"This is why I prefer girls." She groans, looking at her own laptop screen, where a girl's profile is waiting, sans dead animal. "I've never seen a girl on here with a

KIERSTEN MODGLIN

rotting animal body next to her. Fucking poachers."
She slams the laptop closed, leaning back against the
couch with her arms crossed over her chest. "How'd
your date last night go, by the way?"

I roll my eyes, shaking my head. "Uneventful."

"That's never good." She chuckles. "I assumed as
much when you were home before I got off work."

"Yeah. He was fine, he just…" I heave a sigh. "He
wouldn't stop talking about Pokémon."

She's still for a moment, her face visibly processing
what I've said as her eyes dart back and forth between
mine. "*Pokémon?*"

I smile slightly, though I guess it's more of a wince.
"He was so nice. I feel bad. It's just…" I sigh, covering
my face. "Jaz, he brought cards and everything.
Which, like, whatever if that's your thing, but he
somehow made everything about Pokémon. Ev-ery-
thing. Like, 'Oh, this salmon kind of reminds me of
Magikarp' and 'What Pokémon do you think would
choose to live in Nashville?' It was interesting, to say
the least."

Her eyes are wide as she listens to me, actively
fighting the growing smile on her face. "Mm-hmm.
Sounds riveting," she says with a twinkle of humor in
her voice. "Which Pokémon did you decide would be
best suited for the swarm of Broadway bachelorettes?"

I snort. "A musical one, of course. I can't remember
which one he chose. It was multiple choice, and I got it
wrong, obviously."

"Obviously." She beams. "What happened after dinner?"

"He was texting with his friends who were apparently throwing a party, and he wanted me to come, but I wasn't really in the mood to *party*." I shimmy my shoulders sarcastically, which earns me a chuckle.

"I can't imagine why not."

"So I just came home."

"Are you going to see him again?"

"Not if I can help it," I tell her as Simon jumps up on my lap, practically on cue. I pet his head as he rubs his face against my cheek, purring. "Sometimes I think I'm just going to give up the whole dating scene and stay here with my best man."

She snatches the gray cat from me, pulling him onto her lap, and he doesn't seem to mind in the slightest. Most days, I'm pretty sure he likes Jaz better than me, but I'd never let her hear me admit it. "Your best *girl* will try not to be offended," she teases.

I swallow at her words, knowing she means it strictly platonically and does not intend to send me into the dark spiral I ended up in after we broke things off. We both—*she*—agreed we were better off as friends and getting too serious would inevitably result in the end of our friendship when we broke up. Which we—*she*—knew would more than likely happen because something like seventy percent of relationships end within the first year, and our friendship was too important to risk.

I sigh, stuffing another chip into my mouth, but I can't help myself. "Eventually my best girl is going to fall in love and get married and tell me and my obese cat to get out of her apartment."

She gasps and covers Simon's ears, looking directly at him as she speaks. "She didn't mean it, Simmony Cricket. You're beautiful just the way you are."

"His vet would have to disagree wholeheartedly." She's already told us to cut out the treats, but after his last appointment, she had us switch his food too. Nothing seems to help. He's fat and happy, and I love the little rebel for it.

"She needs to step into 2024, doesn't she?" She nods against Simon's nose. "Where we embrace bodies at every size."

I laugh and look away, picking up my phone to see that I have a text from Dominic.

"Oooh. Is that Ash Ketchum?" Jaz asks, leaning over slightly to see my screen.

I ignore the message and my roommate-slash-best friend, and open my dating app again. There has to be someone better out there than what I've been finding lately. "I'm freaking pan. I'm, like, literally the most unpicky sexual orientation there is. How is it that I'm still not able to find someone decent?"

She shrugs. "Well, once you've had the best—" There's a wink that sends a wave through my stomach, and I roll my eyes, looking away and pretending to be annoyed. It doesn't matter. Jaz knows me better than anyone, which is exactly why us being together is a terrible idea.

I toss the bag of chips at her. "I'm going to take a shower." I stop and point at her. "Do not feed my fat cat chips."

She looks away with a mischievous smirk, hugging Simon to her chest and scratching behind his ears just the way he likes. "Wouldn't dream of it. Isn't that right my little Per-Simmon?"

In my hand, my phone vibrates, and I look down to see a message from a new match on my dating app. *And so we begin again.*

CHAPTER THIRTEEN

5—2:23:18

When the next morning rolls around, I have a plan. Albeit it's not a great one, but it's my best attempt. When the guard comes in, while he's unpacking my meal and gathering my trash, I'm going to try to slip the key ring off his belt. Last time, I noticed he has the equivalent of a janitor's set of keys—maybe a dozen of them—on a key ring that's attached to one of those metal carabiner clip things. If I can unhook it from his belt loop without him noticing, once he leaves and locks the door—which he won't need the key for since the key part of the lock is on my side, not his—I'll wait a few minutes, then make a run for it.

I've considered making a run for it when he is inside and walks away from the door, but he always keeps himself in between it and me. If I were to run, I'd have to go past him and be faster. Stealing the keys feels like a safer option, though none of the options feel entirely safe.

In the bathroom, I strip out of my clothes and step into the shower. Aside from the fact that I'm in an unfamiliar shower with none of my usual products, this is the one thing that still feels normal about my routine. I'm usually not one to wash my hair every day —I'm more of an every-third-day gal—but here, I find peace in the methodical scrubbing of my scalp, the rinsing off of sweat, stress, and worry, if only for a moment.

Besides, the unfortunate truth is, if my plan today fails and I make him angry, if he catches me trying to steal his keys or trying to break out of the apartment, there's a good chance this could be my last shower ever.

I swallow at that thought, forcing it away. I can't think like that. I'm going to be smarter than that. Stronger. I'm going to—

The bathroom door flings out, and I screech, grabbing the shower curtain to cover myself as I jerk it back to catch the intruder.

Only...I can't believe my eyes.

"Elliot?"

He stands there staring at me as if he's seen a ghost, his face suddenly ashen, mouth agape. Then he says the last thing I ever expected him to say. "Where *were* you?"

"What do you mean, where was I? Where were *you*?" I grab a towel from the wall and wrap it around myself, stepping out of the shower and stalking toward him.

He shakes his head fervently. "No. I was right here!" He jabs his finger down toward the floor. "I woke up, and you were gone. Where did you go, Sophie? What the hell kind of game are you playing right now?" He shoves his finger toward me in the air, his fingertip nearly connecting with my shoulder.

I ease his hand away from my shoulder with a stony face. "Okay, A, don't scream at me, and don't point at me, and B, I have no idea what you're talking about. I was here. I've *been* here. I haven't left the apartment. I woke up, and you were gone. I searched for you everywhere. I thought I was dreaming." I pause, looking away from him with a sudden worry. "I thought I'd dreamed you up. I thought I'd dreamed the entire day up." *Am I dreaming right now?* I touch his arm cautiously as if he's a science project, and he stares down at the place where our skin connects.

"What are you doing?"

"I don't know that this isn't a dream."

"Right." He's skeptical, clearly.

"I'm serious. How else do you explain it?"

"You think we were both dreaming? Because I also woke up here, and you weren't anywhere to be found. I looked everywhere for you."

"But this could be the dream version of you saying that," I tell him, only half kidding.

He crosses his arms, clearly unamused. "Are you

ever serious? What the fuck is going on here, Soph? How could we have both disappeared? I promise you, I woke up, and you were gone. We both lived the same day but in…alternate universes." He covers his temples with his palms, mussing his hair. "Oh my god. I'm losing my mind. This is it. This is how it all goes down, isn't it?"

"Shut up. This is literally impossible." I shake my head, not understanding. How on earth could what he's saying be true? He couldn't have looked for me. I looked for him. "We aren't both losing our minds simultaneously."

"How do you know?"

"Because I'd never be lucky enough to witness your demise. The universe is never that good to me."

He wrinkles his nose and upper lip, mocking me.

"Maybe they're drugging us. Maybe they kept you in here for a day and moved me somewhere else, and then did the same to you."

"Why would they do that?"

"I have no idea," I admit. "Why would they do any of this? For all I know, this is some weird psychological experiment." The more I think about it, the more likely it seems. After all, they could be changing the count-down clock or stopping it entirely. Every time we fall asleep, we risk them doing something to mess with us. But what are we supposed to do, then? Not sleep? Not eat? The food yesterday never made me sick or sleepy, but now with this new information, everything is on the table again.

"Like something to do with virtual reality?" he asks, lowering his hands away from his head to look around the room with a spacey gleam to his eyes. "Maybe we're not in the apartment at all. Maybe this is all a simulation." He touches the counter thoughtfully, then runs a hand along the wall. "Do you...do you think they're going to kill us?" he asks, turning his head to look at me abruptly. It's the question that has been in the back of my mind and on the tail of every thought since I arrived.

"I try not to think about it, to be honest." I slip past him and into the bedroom. Stopping, I hold up a finger before shutting the door so I can change back into my clothes. "Don't follow me."

He does as I've said, speaking through the door. "I'm sorry I barged in, by the way. The sound of the shower woke me up, but I'd fallen asleep in bed, so I was confused about why I was on the couch and who was in the shower. I didn't actually expect to find you."

Once my clothes are on, I swing the door back open, my hands out to my sides like I'm a circus performer. "Well, ta-da, you did. It's not like it's anything you haven't seen before."

His cheeks flush as he realizes what I've said, and he clears his throat. "We need to come up with a plan." He turns in place as I walk around him to hang up my towel. "Whatever is happening, we have to get out of here."

"I already have a plan," I tell him.

"And that is?" He eyes me.

I open my mouth to tell him, but something stops me. I don't know if it's distrust of him or the fact that I'm starting to wonder if we might be under surveillance. Especially if they're waiting for us to fall asleep to do whatever trickery they have up their sleeves. Either way, I shake my head. "Just follow my lead, okay?"

He doesn't look like that's enough of an answer, but eventually, he swallows. Then he nods. "Whatever you say."

CHAPTER FOURTEEN

BEFORE — ONE WEEK AGO

Jaz walks past the bathroom with her headphones on, bobbing her head to whatever song she's listening to—probably Beyoncé's new album, since she's had it on repeat lately.

I lean closer into the mirror, swiping a tinted lip balm across my lips before I realize she has backed up. She stands in the bathroom doorway and pulls her headphones down around her neck. She looks me up and down.

"Hot damn. You got a hot date?"

Does she sound jealous? I can't tell.

Do I want her to? I don't know.

I rub my lips together, putting the cap on my lip balm before I turn around and swipe my hands across the floral jumpsuit I'm wearing. I'm going for a sort of comfy, casual look that still feels put together without trying too hard. We're going to walk around the park, but then grab dinner at a bar afterward, so I want to be dressed appropriately for both. "Yeah, maybe. I'm meeting up with that guy I've been talking to."

"Which one?"

"DJ. Remember, the one with the dog?"

She purses her lips. "DJ? There is zero chance in hell you're going to go out with a guy whose nickname could be D, and not hear a joke about"—she lowers her voice to what must be an impression of him—"*wanting the D* within half an hour, an hour max."

I snort. "Oh, please. He seems nice. He's one of the few guys who's kept it strictly professional."

"Oh, good. 'Cause that's what you want. Everything professional. HR papers and fluorescent lighting. Sooo hot."

"You know what I mean," I say with a click of my tongue. "He hasn't been gross, which is saying something. Now, help me. What do you think?"

"Where are you going?" she asks, eyes traveling over my outfit.

I lay out our plans quickly and she nods.

"Yeah, this is cute, then. Are you going to be too hot? Would shorts be better?"

I glance down. "Maybe, but I don't want to look too casual. Or show too much leg."

She rolls her eyes, but not at me. At the world. I'm used to it. "Right, 'cause heaven forbid a woman show extra skin." She clutches her imaginary pearls. "Oh, it's a knee! Whatever will the townsfolk say?"

I press my lips together, hiding my laughter. She's not wrong. "I'll be fine."

She straightens her shoulders. "Yeah, you will." Then she winks. "Big D won't know what hit him."

I groan loudly, then shove her out of the room with a laugh. "You're the literal worst."

"You love me," she calls through the door.

Yeah, I do.

CHAPTER FIFTEEN

5 — 2:21:18

The plan is in motion when I hear the man outside the door, the timing throwing everything off. We've hidden pillows under the blankets in the bed so it looks like we're sleeping if anyone comes to check, the same way I did when I was a teenager and sneaking out. I'm not sure it's convincing, but it's the best we can do.

And though there are no visible cameras, if someone is watching us, they probably saw us doing it anyway and have figured out our plan. Suddenly, I'm second-guessing myself and paranoid about everything.

We were supposed to be hidden under the bed when they came in, so we could catch them doing whatever they had planned, but now we don't have time to cross the room before the man enters the apartment.

This time he does it with his gun already in hand.

My blood runs cold at the sight. I'd forgotten about the gun. I stand, hands in the air.

"We aren't going to do anything," I promise him.

"Stay back," he warns.

I nod and do as he says as Elliot comes to stand next to me. The man keeps his head turned toward us as he sets the box down and begins to unpack it. When he's finished and puts the lid back on the box, I point to the fridge, reverting to my original plan and crossing my fingers it works. "We have some trash this time, too." I gesture for him to go and get it.

He jabs the gun in the air toward the fridge. "Bring it to me."

"Oh." I swallow, meeting Elliot's eyes. "Okay, do you mind getting it for him?"

Elliot starts to walk forward, but the man holds out the gun to stop him. Determination and curiosity weigh on Elliot's features like he knows something is up, though I'm not sure he's figured out what it is.

"No. *Her.*" He wiggles the gun in the air, forcing me to make my way toward the fridge. I turn back just once, flicking my eyes to Elliot's, then toward the man's waist, wishing I'd told him the plan and hoping he'll understand what I'm saying. "Open it," the man orders, his weapon trained on me.

I do. Working quickly and with shaking hands, I pull the food tray out. With everything in me, I'm trying not to show him how nervous I am. I spin around, holding out the tray.

"Now bag it up. There are trash bags under the sink." The man jabs his gun in that direction.

I open one of the doors under the sink and grab a black trash bag, shoving the food inside of it and tying it up. It seems like an awful waste of plastic to just put a few things inside of it, and I know now that Jaz is rubbing off on me because I never would've thought of that before we met.

When I hold it out, he snatches the bag from me and puts it into the box with a huff, then turns toward the door, gun pointed at us as he backs out of it.

As we hear the door lock, I release a sigh. "Well, so much for my plan."

When I look at Elliot, though, he's grinning ear to ear. "Oh, I don't know. I think it worked pretty well." He lifts his hand to reveal the key ring clad with keys.

I gasp. I could literally kiss him right now. *I won't, obviously*, but it's a thought. My first thought, which is disturbing. *Ew. Get it together, Soph.* I jump up on my tiptoes. "Holy cow! How did you manage to get those?"

He grins wickedly. "Same way you were planning to, I'm guessing. When he was distracted watching you get the food, I eased them off his clip. You forget that I know you pretty well, Sophie. Even if you don't trust me enough to tell me what the plan was, I could figure it out."

I won't deny that I don't trust him anymore. He's given me no reason to, not when he left and not now. On a cellular level, I do trust him because my body knows him as the little boy I grew up with and the teenager I fell in love with, but there's also a part of me closer to the surface that watched him walk away from me. A part of me he broke and hardened that might never be able to trust him again.

"So, now what?" I ask, my throat dry.

He squeezes his palm around the keys. "We need to leave. Now. If he figures out we took them, he'll be back."

I nod. "Right. Okay." Suddenly the idea of escaping is overwhelming. Right now, though we certainly aren't safe, we're not in active danger. If we walk out that door, everything could change. He could be waiting for us to do exactly what we've done. He could hurt us, kill us even. This could be a trap that we've walked all too willingly into.

"Are you ready?" Elliot's Adam's apple bobs with a hard swallow, and he looks me up and down.

"Wait. We should make sure he's gone." I rush across the room and move the curtains back, peering out the window just in time to see a golf cart disappearing into the tree line.

He's gone.

At least for the moment, he's gone. Now's our chance. Maybe our only chance.

"We need to go." Elliot appears behind me, staring out the window over my shoulder.

Still, even knowing that he's right, it takes several seconds for me to agree, but what choice do we have?

We can't stay here, awaiting our fate, waiting for one of us to disappear again. Whatever is going on, I have to try. I have to fight.

So I give a heavy nod and walk toward the door with him as a funny thought hits me. What if we walk out of here to a soundstage? What if the windows are computer screens showing us whatever the man wants us to see? What if we're Jim Carrey in some weird *Truman Show* scenario?

He tries several keys, each one stealing a bit of my hope away like a leaf on the wind. Finally, when one key twists in the lock, he glances back at me with wide eyes and a determined look before pulling the door open. I wince, half expecting a loud alarm to blare, but nothing happens. Instead, I shield my eyes from the bright sunshine of freedom, wincing as he opens the storm door.

My heart pounds in my chest, ramming itself against my ribcage like a rabid dog trying to escape its pen. I can't believe it was this easy. It shouldn't have been this easy, and yet, here we are. Free.

Well, almost.

Sort of.

I pull the door shut behind us and make sure to lock it back before hurrying down the concrete stairs that lead to the building. It's a house we've been in, not an apartment, I realize once I have my first good look at it. It's small, probably around five hundred square feet, and there's no driveway leading up to it. The house has been plopped in the middle of the woods with no discernible path to get here. It's quite charming, actually. There are no signs of the prison on the inside from the outside. The cottage is small and singular, painted robin's egg blue with white shutters around the small windows. There are three concrete steps with a metal railing on one side, and all around us, even farther than I could see from the windows, there are only trees.

It's like nothing beyond this place exists.

Like Hansel and Gretel, we've been trapped in a storybook house in the middle of the woods, and we have no idea when the wicked witch might be coming back for us.

Around us, birds chirp and the wind blows, and everything feels entirely too quiet and calm compared to the storm raging inside me.

"Come on," he insists, holding out his hand to bring me back to reality.

I slip my palm into his and launch myself forward with him by my side, running at full speed toward the trees. "He went this way," I tell him, slowing down as we near the tree line, and the sudden fear that the man might be waiting just behind a tree crosses my mind.

The world is silent around us, only the sound of our cautious footsteps crunching over twigs and leaves as we move farther across the grass and safely under the cover of the trees. Our ragged breaths fill my ears as we move, tiptoeing to a safety still not guaranteed.

Once inside the forest, there is nothing except a spider web of worn dirt paths.

As we reach the tree line, I stop, grabbing on to a tree with one hand and bending at the waist, gulping air as if it'll be my last chance to do so. Next to me, Elliot stares around, studying the woods.

"I'm not sure which way is the highway. It's so quiet out here." He steps forward, ear tilted in one direction, then the other. "That way, maybe?" He points straight ahead. "It looks like the main route." He swivels around, studying the paths. "It has to lead us somewhere."

He doesn't say out loud the part I know he's thinking. The part about how it might lead us straight into danger. Directly to our captor.

"What do you think?"

"We'll stay within the trees," I tell him when I've mostly caught my breath. "Move slowly and quietly. Eventually, we'll find a way to escape, and until then"— I look his way, suddenly feeling vulnerable—"we'll stick together."

He rubs his lips together. "We'll be fine," he assures me, then turns to face me completely, his hands on my shoulders. "I'm not going to let anything happen to you, Soph. I promise."

Something burns in the back of my throat over his words and the way he's looking at me. Once, he looked at me this way often, but now I don't have time to dwell on it. I don't have time or energy to reminisce or wonder what could've been because it isn't.

We're going to get through this. Together. That's all I need to focus on. I take a step back, and he drops his hands, allowing me to face the direction we're heading as we take our first few steps that way.

The weather is stiflingly hot as we make our way down the path. I pull my shirt out away from my chest, fanning myself. I don't know what to think or expect, and I find myself drifting back to Jaz, wondering what she's doing right now. I know whatever she must imagine has happened to me, it won't be this. Walking through a mysterious forest with my ex-boyfriend wouldn't be high on my list of guesses if I were in her shoes, either.

We're quiet as we go, lost in our own thoughts and listening for any signs we're being chased or coming up on the man, wherever he is. I know as soon as he finds out we're missing, he'll be looking for us right where we are. The forest is the only place we could go, so there's no doubt he'll find us if he wants to unless we're faster and smarter than he is. That's not likely, though. Surely, he knows the woods better than we do. He knows where to go and where not to. And it's possible he has help, too.

I hope we'll have the full twenty-four hours to run before he plans to bring us tomorrow's food, but in reality, I know even an hour is cutting it. How long will it take for him to realize he doesn't have his keys? How soon will he need them again? And when he does, how serious will he be about finding us? What will he do to us if he does?

Questions swarm in my mind like bees to a hive, buzzing about as I run, refusing to give me even a moment's peace. The forest is thicker here, more laden with trees and brush, so we have to move slower. Moisture clings to my skin and clothes, making the heat so suffocating I'm having trouble catching my breath.

As something comes into view up ahead, my heart picks up speed. We're nearly there. Wherever *there* is, we've nearly found it.

Then...*no*.

We stop in our tracks at nearly the same time. Elliot's eyes land on me, then back behind us. "It's impossible." His voice is breathy and exhausted.

"We've gone in circles." Somehow, we ended up right back at the house. We've made absolutely no progress at all. The house sits up ahead of us, waiting to welcome us home.

I turn, rage filling my chest like a balloon ready to burst as I make my way back down the path and find a new one to take. Elliot jogs to keep up with me, breathing heavily. Again, a Hansel and Gretel reference fills my mind as I wish we'd brought the crackers from our dinner with us to leave a marked path and whittle down our options. Everything looks the same out here. It's nothing but trees and brush. The paths are all overgrown, and there are plenty that I can't tell whether they're paths at all.

We take a turn on a path I'm certain we haven't taken previously, and I note a large, fallen log off to the left.

"We haven't seen that before, right?" I point to it, drawing Elliot's attention.

He huffs. "I don't remember." Then, quickly, he adds, "I don't think so."

But soon enough, I feel my heart flutter, then slam to the ground with undeniable weight. "No." Bitterness rises in my chest like helium. "It's impossible."

"You were right. We *are* going in circles," Elliot says, staring up at the house ahead of us with a pinched expression. "Everything looks exactly the same. All of the paths must lead to the same place."

"The man went this way." Anger bubbles out of me. "At least one of these paths must lead somewhere different. We just have to find the right one."

I turn and hurry backward without waiting for him to agree. I'm not going to give in. Not yet. I turn down the next path, digging my shoes in the dirt to leave marks.

"You'll lead him right to us," Elliot says, trying to keep up, though he's clearly exhausted. So am I, though I seem to be fueled by stubbornness, spurred on by my refusal to give up.

Spinning around to see the tracks I'm leaving, my body turns cold when I realize he's right. The footprints, meant to save us, could also be the thing that endangers us. Running back, I brush away the footprints until there's no trace of them. "It doesn't matter," I grumble, angry with myself for not thinking it through and with Elliot for being right.

"It's for the best. We don't need to leave a trail for him to follow. There are only so many paths for us to try. Come on, keep going," Elliot says, rushing me forward.

After we've followed the fourth path and ended up right back at the house where we started, when my lungs are burning and begging for air, and my heart is pounding so hard I'm afraid it might give out, Elliot finally stops, gasping for breaths of his own. He rests his back against a nearby tree, head pointed toward the sky, hand on his chest. "This isn't working," he says between gulps of air. "Everything looks the same. We have to think of another way to do this. Maybe we should split up."

"No," I say quickly. "That's even worse. I'd rather be lost together than alone."

"Okay, fine. What about this path?" He points to a different, worn path ahead. One that looks exactly the same as all the others. "Have we gone this way?"

I shake, clutching my chest as my heart pounds underneath my fingers, proof that I'm still alive and fighting. Proof that this isn't all in my head. "I don't think so."

He runs a hand through his hair. "We don't have

much longer before he figures out that we're missing. Only so many more chances."

"I know. It's starting to get dark, too. That isn't helping." I'm just realizing it, but the sky around us has dimmed to a gray, and the forest is cloaked in more shadows than it was earlier. We're going to have to spend the night here if we don't make it out soon. Even if we keep moving, we're going to be cast into the dark of the night here without a choice before long. We need to find somewhere safe to hide, should it come to that. A cave, maybe, or at least the base of a large tree. Maybe we could even find one with a hollow big enough for us to hide inside. I just refuse to go back to that house.

"Wait." His eyes lock on something up ahead, and he suddenly takes off, jogging forward. "Look! This path." He wags a finger at a small, overgrown path next to a fallen tree. "Up here. I don't think we've tried this way."

I can't see what it is or where he's going—in fact, I'm not even completely sure it *is* a path—but I follow blindly, willing to try anything. At first, everything feels very similar to the other paths we've taken, but when I spot a post ahead, something tightens in my chest.

The post isn't marked, and we could've easily overlooked it before, but this feels different. We haven't been this way. Somehow, I just know it.

He seems to sense it, too, as he picks up his pace.

When we reach the destination, he stops short, and I nearly slam into him. "What is it?"

In an instant, he backtracks, hand over my mouth as he pushes me to hide behind a tree. When he answers, he keeps his voice low. "Shh. Look." He points ahead, and I peek my head around the tree, trying to see what he's talking about.

Up ahead, nearly camouflaged by the many trees, there is a tall, barbed-wire fence blocking our way out. The metal wires are much too close together to even try climbing over or through, but if that wasn't bad enough, there's a man pacing in front of the gate with a gun resting on his hip. I can't tell if this is the same man from earlier or someone different.

He looks almost like a soldier. Or a prison guard.

I duck back behind the tree, heart racing. A breath escapes my lips as I process what I'm seeing.

Even after we escaped, we're still trapped.

CHAPTER SIXTEEN

BEFORE — ONE WEEK AGO

> Fucking men

I send the text to Jaz right before flagging down the waitress, who is probably glad to finally see me giving up. She's been by five times in the last hour to check on me, and I can tell she figured out I was being stood up even before I did.

I should've, in hindsight. Clearly.

My date, DJ, hasn't answered the text I sent him about twenty-three minutes past the point we said we were going to be meeting. He's been so kind since we started talking that I truly wanted to give him the benefit of the doubt. I thought traffic or a family emergency or work had kept him late. I wanted to believe everything except the possibility that he'd stood me up, but now, the truth is undeniable.

What sort of loser waits a full hour for a date she's never even met in person before?

Then again, maybe he did actually come. Maybe he came and saw me and realized I was uglier than my profile picture would lead you to believe, and he ditched me. Not that I'm one of those girls who puts super-edited pictures on their profile, but I definitely choose my best ones. Today, it's miserably hot, so my normally sleek, brown hair is frizzy, with an annoying bottom layer of perfect spiral curls near the back of my neck that won't translate to the rest of my head no matter how hard I try. My makeup is probably cakey, and my eyeliner is undoubtedly gathered in the corners and creases of my eyes.

Today, thinking sitting outside on the patio would make me look cool and not like a swamp witch was likely one of many mistakes.

> He didn't show?

> Nope. Haven't heard a word from him.

> Jerk. His loss. Come home. I found this new show where a bunch of actors convince this one guy he's on a jury, even though it's all fake. It's hilarious.

I slip my phone into my pocket, signing the bill the waitress brought over before standing up and dropping cash on the table for a tip.

Outside the restaurant, I open my phone to order an Uber and press the button at the crosswalk.

"Sophie?" an out-of-breath voice calls to me, drawing my attention to the sidewalk next to me where a man stands.

He's red-faced, and his temples are as sweaty as mine feel. He's got floppy, brown hair like that popular '90s haircut à la Shawn Hunter and Uncle Jesse— except not when he had the mullet—and green eyes. He's older than the guys I usually date, early thirties, and has a bit of a five o'clock shadow I didn't see in any of his pictures. Still, I know it's him.

Like me, he seems to be one of the only people on dating apps who uses real photos. It's refreshing, honestly. Then again, he clearly doesn't need to use fake photos. He's easily one of the most attractive men I've ever seen, even in his current damp state. My breathing catches in my throat at the sight of him, and I try desperately not to let it show.

I cross my arms over my chest. "Sorry, do I know you?"

He winces. "Oh, did I not tell you my name? I'm Asshole."

"Asshole?" I snort, raising a brow.

He draws one corner of his mouth in. "Yeah, it's a whole thing. My parents are proctologists."

I nod, slightly amused by his antics. "Mm-hmm. And naturally they wanted to honor that."

He grins. "You think I got the raw end of the deal, but you should meet my brother, Anal Leakage."

At that, I snort-laugh, covering my mouth as my cheeks flame.

He drops the act then, his face going sincere. "Seriously, I'm so sorry I'm late. I spilled something on my shirt at work, so I had to run to the store to buy a new one because I didn't have time to go all the way home. Then someone stole my phone at the store, so I had to report it, and it was..." He huffs a sigh. "A nightmare, to put it lightly, but I'm so sorry I'm late. I didn't even have time to get a new phone. I just knew I'd missed you, but I had to try. I can't believe you waited."

"I ran into a friend, and it gave us a chance to catch up." I wave him off with a complete lie. "No big deal."

"Oh." He blinks, looking toward the restaurant. "Okay, good. Well, does that mean you're not hungry? I'd still love to have dinner or drinks if you're up for it."

I pretend to contemplate. "Sure, but somewhere else, if that's okay. Since I already used our reservation." If I go in there, there's a really big chance the waitress will make a comment that makes me seem too pathetic.

"Okay, cool. I'm DJ, by the way. The Asshole thing was a joke. Obviously."

"Too bad. I was really looking forward to introducing you to people." A smile plays on my lips as our light changes, and we cross the street, both of us fighting against looking at each other as we try to play it cool.

CHAPTER SEVENTEEN

3—1:18:42

"We have to go back." Elliot's hushed voice draws me out of my panic before I turn my head to look at him.

"Back?"

"Back." He nods, taking a step backward. "Back to the house. We'll…" He chews his lip, clearly thinking aloud. "We'll leave the keys outside the door, so he'll just think he dropped them, but we'll keep the key to the house. And then tomorrow we can break out again with supplies to help us get through this. We know where the fence is now. We know it's guarded here, but we can move along the trees and look for a safer place to escape. We know the correct path, but we can't do it without supplies. Blankets, scissors, or pliers maybe. Whatever we can find. We'll know the way. We can come straight back here." His eyes search mine as he waits for me to respond.

"But why? We found the way out. We can't just give up."

He glares at me. "The man is armed, and it's getting dark. Even without all of that working against us, do you have any idea about how to get over that fence?" His hand waves toward the fence that I clearly can't scale without destroying my body in the process. "Because unless you do, we can't get through there, and the longer we're gone, the more chance we risk of them figuring out what we've done and searching for us. If we stay here, we may as well be trapped rats." He sighs, pinching the skin of his nose. "Look, I want to get out of here as badly as you do, trust me. But we have to be smart about this."

I scowl, unable to believe he's actually suggesting this. It's the one option that doesn't feel like it's on the table for me. There has to be another way. "And smart is going back to the place that had us trapped in the first place?"

"*Smart* is making a plan that keeps us safe. It's understanding we don't have much longer before it's too dark to see anything. It's knowing that if they realize we're gone, there's a very good chance they're going to kill us." He lowers his voice. "If that guard hears or sees us, they're going to kill us."

"A few days early, you mean."

He lets out a slow breath through his nose. "*Smart* is going back, knowing the way out, and coming back tomorrow with a safe way to make it happen. Don't let your fear make you do something stupid, Soph. Trust me. For once just trust me. Please?"

I hate the conviction in his voice as much as I hate the fact that I think he might be right. I really, really don't want him to be right.

We're here, we made it, and we're still not free.

Blowing a puff of air from my lips, I drop my shoulders, looking around. "Okay. Fine." I don't see that we have any other choice, and I certainly don't want to be alone again. We've found the fence, the path to safety, but if we can't get across it, maybe he's right that we'll be safer coming back tomorrow with materials and supplies. Maybe even food and water, in case we're farther away from civilization than we imagined at first.

For all I know, we could be in the wilderness of Canada. We have to pack things. We were reckless today, drunk on the idea of escaping with no understanding of our surroundings.

I have to be smarter than my impulsive nature would like me to be.

He stares at me, like he thinks I'm going to change my mind, but eventually, I turn, and he follows my lead. On the way, he twists one key off the keychain and tucks it into his pocket.

"Which way was the shortest path back? Do you remember?" I ask when we reach the spider web of paths. The heat has become so overwhelming I can't remember which direction we came from. Not that I've ever been good with directions, no matter the temperature.

I could get lost in my own building, and more than once, I've gotten lost in a store.

He looks this way, then that. "I guess it doesn't matter. They'll all eventually get us back to the house. Let's go this way." He points to a path on our left, and I nod, walking forward.

"It's all so strange, isn't it?" I ask him, filling the silence with our whispers. "I mean, if they wanted to kill us, they could have already done it. What could the countdown be for? What do you think is going to happen when it's over?"

"I don't know that I want to think about it," he admits. "I want to get us out of here and long gone before then."

Quickly enough, and yet all too soon, the house comes into view up ahead, and a storm of feelings swims through me. Rage and hopelessness that we've had to come back, relief that no one is there waiting for us, and, maybe most of all, fear that he might be waiting inside.

"Wait," I tell Elliot when he starts to walk out into the yard, grabbing his arm to stop him. I look around, making sure the man is nowhere to be seen before we take off across the grass and up the stairs. True to his plan, he drops the keys on the grass next to the steps before unlocking our door.

When he does, we step inside, and the hairs on the

back of my neck immediately stand at attention. The space is the same—the same couch, the same curtains, the same coffee table in the center of the room, but something is off.

A scent in the air, perhaps, or the temperature of the room. I look at Elliot to see if he senses it too, but his eyes are on the countdown clock on the far wall. I follow his gaze.

3—1:18:42

I blink, trying to make sense of it. "What the hell? When did it change—"

"Who are you?"

I turn toward the sound of the voice that interrupted me to see an older man standing at the end of the hallway. He's got completely silver hair and a stout frame. Just behind him, there's a man around my age with blond hair and a similar build. They have the same jawline and eyes, and it's impossible to miss. Were they here looking for us? Did they think we'd already escaped?

"What are you doing here?" I demand.

"Are you bringing our food?" the man asks, eyeing us suspiciously.

"Your food?" Elliot asks.

"Yes. It's usually a person in a costume," the older one says, casting a wary glance behind him to the other man, then turning his attention back to us. His eyes travel up and down over Elliot's body. He clears his throat. "Why aren't you wearing the costume?"

All at once, it clicks. The other houses. The different paths.

They weren't ours.

"Your food." I pause. "The man in the black suit of armor brings your food? You're stuck here, too?" I look around, realizing the subtle differences between this house and ours. This one is a bit dirtier, more lived in. The kitchen island has a small chunk of wood missing from the corner that ours doesn't. The light is different here. This isn't the home where we've been kept, but it's eerily similar.

The guy swallows and looks behind him again, checking with the younger man. "Too? You mean you're also being held here by the man dressed in black?"

Elliot and I look at each other before nodding. "Not *here*, but in a house just like this one," I explain. "They're identical from the outside. We've only been here for a day or two so far."

"Do you have any idea what's going on? Where are we?" the man asks.

Elliot shrugs, glancing at me. "We woke up in the house with no idea how we got there. Is that how it went for you guys?"

The man drops his chin with a solemn nod. "I'm… I'm Robert. This is my boy, Nick. How did you manage to get out?"

"Can you get us out, too?" Nick asks, stepping forward with hopeful eyes.

"How long have you been here?" I ask, filled with too many questions. There are others? How are there others? They seem unharmed, but their countdown clock hasn't ended yet…or has it? Have they just reset it, perhaps? There is so much I want to ask them and so little time.

"We've lost track," Robert says. "Just a few days, I think." He glances at the countdown. "We're getting close to that thing being on zero. Is that when they let you out?"

I exchange another glance with Elliot, unsure if we can trust these people, but before either of us can say or do anything, I hear a sound that chills me to my core.

Whistling.

Someone is whistling outside the door. He's back. The man is about to come inside.

Shoot. Shoot. Shoot. Shoot. Shoot.

Ice slips through my veins, and I see it register on Elliot's face at the same moment it does mine.

"Go," Robert whispers, sensing our panic and waving a hand over his shoulder. "Go hide in the bedroom."

Without needing to be told twice, we dart past him and down the hallway just in time for the door to swing open. Our footsteps quiet into near silence as we sneak into the bedroom to see the neatly made bed and two sets of shoes thrown in the corner. I look at the closet, but opening the door risks making too much noise.

Under the bed is our only option, so we go for it, scrambling across the carpet into the small space. Once we're there and settled, I try to slow my racing heart with easy, steady breaths. I need to be able to hear what's going on so we're ready for whatever comes next.

CHAPTER EIGHTEEN

3—1:18:31

The space under the bed isn't comfortable, and I'm fighting everything in me not to panic as my claustrophobia sets in. The metal bars are touching my back, and with my front on the carpet, I feel as if I can't breathe properly.

Next to me, Elliot slides his hand into mine as if he can sense my anxiety levels rising. I'm not positive, but I think it might be the first time he's touched me since he woke me up stumbling over the dishes the day he arrived. I don't know what to do with it. We're face down on the carpeted floor with the bed providing very little cover should the man walk into the room right now.

If he knows we're here, this is the first place he'll look. I'm certain of it.

Somehow, despite the worry in my gut and the confusion over my feelings for Elliot, his hand in mine does just what I need. It's a balm for my fears, a promise that no matter what happens, we're in this together.

He's grounding me without any idea he's doing it. Without any idea I needed it so badly.

I turn my head and rest my cheek against the carpet, meeting his eyes as we listen to the hushed voices down the hall. It sounds like he's delivering food to them, just like he has been for us, though I hear no threats for them. I guess they've been better behaved.

I smile to myself thinking of how I attacked the man that first day, and though he doesn't know what I'm smiling about, Elliot grins back.

Eventually, the door shuts and the sounds of footsteps rushing our way freezes my heart in my chest. I swear I black out, because one second the footsteps are coming, and the next, the man is on the floor at the end of the bed, nodding and waving for me to come out.

"It's alright. He's gone. You're safe." He nods and waves, coaxing us out of hiding as Elliot lets go of my hand and begins to slide out from under the bed.

I crawl out on the other side, dusting off the front of my clothes before meeting the eyes of the man and his son, who both look equally as terrified as we are.

"Are you okay?" the man asks me.

I check with Elliot before answering. "Yes, I think so. Thank you for hiding us."

He presses his lips together, the skin around his blue eyes wrinkling with concern. "What are you doing here? You still haven't told us. How did you even get here?"

Elliot holds up the key. "We escaped. Tried to run, but there's a fence around the entire property, watched by at least one armed guard. We were coming back for supplies, and we thought this was the house they'd been keeping us in. Like she said earlier, they look exactly alike."

The man presses his lips together, trying to understand. "So, wait a minute, there are more places than just this one? How did you manage to find us? How many others are there?"

"We don't know. The woods are thick all around the houses. It's easy to get lost out there. We took several paths and kept ending up back at the house we thought was ours, but if they were all different, there's easily a half dozen or so." I glance toward the window, then back. "Do you know the man who has us here? Who he is, I mean. Have you seen his face?"

He shakes his head, looking at his son, who agrees. "My son was missing for two days before I was brought here," he says. "I don't remember anything about how I got here, other than waking up and being in the same house. A house neither of us recognize. The man has brought us food every day, but always with his face covered, and I assume he's disguising his voice. Sometimes it sounds a bit deeper than others, and I think there's been a hint of an accent a few times he's spoken."

"And you?" I turn to the son. "You don't know him either?"

"No," he says quickly. "Same as Dad. I woke up here. I was brutally sick the first day. I pretty much thought I was dying, but then…I just got better. I don't know how to explain it. And then I woke up, and Dad was here."

"And you don't remember how you got here? Did you go out with friends or…" I trail off, searching my own memory for answers to the same questions.

"I don't know," Nick says with a sigh. "I really don't. I mean, maybe, but ever since we had our second baby, I'm home more than ever. I just really don't remember if I was out or why I would've been. I've tried really hard to think back, but it's like there's fog in my head. It's all blurry." His eyes search the air, like the answer to all our problems might just be there waiting for us to find it. Then they land on me. "What about you? Do you remember what happened? How you got here?"

I shake my head. "It's the same for—"

A sound in the living room interrupts us, and before I have time to process what's happening, the door opens. Elliot and I dart toward the bed, scrambling to get underneath it as Robert and Nick rush down the hall. The carpet burns my arms as I scoot to safety as quickly as I can.

"Where are they?" the man shouts, and something inside me shatters.

This is it.

This is it.

This is it.

It's all over.

Robert cries out in what sounds like pain, but it could just be fear. "What are you talking about?" He's not convincing in the least, and I wince, hoping the man is just looking for something—anything—other than us.

"I know they're in here," the man shouts, his voice gruff. I hear Nick whimper, then he cries out, and I assume the worst. He's hurt him somehow or pulled the gun out. "Tell me or your boy gets it. Plain and simple, old man. Don't be a hero."

"Please don't," Nick begs, his voice trembling.

"Stop! Please. In there," Robert reveals without hesitation. "They're in there. Under the bed. We didn't know they were coming. Please believe us."

My brain flickers, vision blurring as the boots come into view. A hand grabs my arm, and I don't try to fight back. What's the point?

Before I know what's happening, I'm out from under the bed and the man is standing in front of me. Though I can't see his eyes through the plastic of his mask, I know he's staring at me with fury. I can practically feel the heat radiating off of him. He's shaking as he holds me. Elliot is out next, scrambling to stand beside me.

"It was my fault," he says. "I forced her to leave. It was me."

"Shut up!" the man shouts, whacking him in the side head with his gun.

Elliot cries out, clasping a hand over the place on his temple where he was hit.

Without another word, the man points the gun in my direction and forces us out of the room. In the kitchen, Robert and Nick are huddled together, and I spot a bloody gash on Nick's forehead.

I don't look at Robert. I can't. He owed us nothing, and that's exactly what he gave us. What right do I have to be mad at him? I'm the reason his son was hurt. I'm the reason he was threatened. And yet, I am mad.

I'm furious, in fact. Angrier with them than even the captor.

Jaz always gets mad at me for this. I'm a giver. I give and do for people, whether or not I know them. I've been scammed by so many crowdfunding ploys, I can't even count. I'm always the first to do for my family, just for them to turn around and ignore me. So I can say without hesitation that I would've protected Robert and his son without them having to ask. I would've done that, but they didn't do the same for me. It's a hard pill to swallow every single time.

Even in a situation as rare and unique as this, I still found a way to be let down.

We walk through the small living room with the man close behind us, and when we reach the door, I stop.

"Go," he prompts. "Open the door."

Slowly, I reach out my hand for the doorknob, wondering if it will be unlocked or if he'll expect me to use the key we stole. Has he figured out that we stole it? How did he know we were here in the first place? The question occurs to me for the first time. How could he have possibly known?

As our time in this place passes, I'm filled with so many more questions than answers.

A glance over my shoulder tells me the countdown clock on the wall now says

3—1:18:31

Robert and Nick only have one more day here. What happens then? What will they do to them? Will they let them go? Doubtful. What happens when our time runs out shortly after theirs? I'm too terrified to try to guess.

"Go!" he bellows, and I feel the cool metal of the gun pressed into my spine.

I turn the knob, and to my relief, the door opens without the key. It wasn't locked. He leads us down the stairs where there is a golf cart waiting. As a kid, I loved these things. Now I'm not sure I'll ever look at one the same way. If I'm lucky enough to get the chance to see one again. For all I know, he's taking us somewhere to be killed like the problem children we clearly are.

I turn to look at him, and he lifts up his free hand,

locking the door behind him before walking down the stairs and pulling a set of handcuffs out of his pocket. I hadn't noticed them before, but somehow, they don't surprise me.

I'm not sure anything could surprise me anymore.

He holds them out without a word.

"What do you want from us?" I ask, stopping Elliot as he goes to hold out his hands willingly.

The man nudges the cuffs toward us, still not speaking, and slaps one end on Elliot's wrist, then gestures toward the golf cart. When Elliot sits down on the back, he attaches the other cuff to the opposite side.

With his attention turned away from me, I lean forward and search for a way to escape. Could I try to take the gun away from him? Considering I have no idea how to use one even if I could get it away from him, I'm not sure that's wise. I could make a run for it, but I'd never leave my idiot ex-boyfriend alone, and even if I could stomach the thought of doing that, my chances of getting away from a man with a golf cart and gun don't feel that promising. Not to mention that we're fenced in, and we can now assume there are other guards with guns just waiting for us to try to escape.

As he pulls out a new set of handcuffs, I'm clearly up next, but when the cuffs are on my wrist and I move around to sit next to Elliot on the back seat, the man shakes his head. "Nice try. You're next to me."

I swallow. The last thing I want to do right now is

sit next to this man while he drives us to god knows where to do god knows what, but I do as I'm told and wince as he attaches me to the side of the cart. I can feel Elliot's stare burning into me as he watches us from over his shoulder, but I don't dare look at him. Instead, I keep my eyes locked straight ahead as the man comes to sit next to me and turns the key in the cart's ignition.

He backs us away from the house and toward the woods, and I catch a hint of his unfamiliar scent on the breeze. It's musky and warm, like sweat and fried food. When we reach the tree line, he turns toward a path with a clear sense of where we're going.

"Where are you taking us?" I ask. To be punished, I can only assume.

He tightens his grip on the steering wheel without answering.

"How many of us are there? How many more houses?"

That at least gets me a look in my direction, and he fires back a question of his own. "How did you get the key?"

I look straight ahead again. "I don't know what you mean."

He picks up speed in the golf cart so the little engine is whirring.

"How. Did you get. The key?" he repeats through what sounds like gritted teeth.

"We never had a key. You left the door unlocked,"

Elliot says, turning in his seat to face us the best he can with his arm attached to the pole behind him. "On your way out. Must've been distracted."

"Bullshit," the man mutters under his breath.

"Where are you taking us?" I ask him again as we take another turn.

"Home." His answer is simple yet anything but.

"Home where?" I demand. "Where are we?"

"We're home, Sophie. You're home." And something about the sound of my name on his lips sends my insides into a violent rage. When we see the little robin's egg blue house come into view with its picturesque white shutters and a small number five next to the door, my stomach churns for an entirely new reason. I lurch forward, holding my stomach and leaning over the side of my seat just in time for the vomit to spew out of my mouth.

This place will never be my home. I refuse to live here any longer. More than that, I refuse to die here.

I wipe my mouth with the back of my hand, squaring my shoulders with more determination than I've felt since I arrived. Somehow, I'm going to go home.

CHAPTER NINETEEN

BEFORE — ONE WEEK AGO

He laughs, and I like it. It's charming somehow, and I am rarely charmed, especially by guys who nearly stand me up on our first date.

"Okay, okay," he says through his laughter. "Well, fine. If you want to get technical, I guess you could say it's frowned upon, but I'm just saying you can literally put as much butter and cheese as you want on, like, everything. Absolutely no one regulates it."

I chuckle, shaking my head as he puts more parmesan cheese on his spaghetti. "My best friend is vegan, so we don't keep the real stuff in the house, and I tend to go a little overboard when I'm away."

He pushes the plate of uni butter toward me, then the basket of bread. "Overboard." His lips twist with a wry grin. "Was that a play on this nautical-themed appetizer?" he asks with a chuckle, pointing his knife toward the butter.

I don't need a reminder that I'm literally eating sea urchin testicles, but I smile anyway. "Not intentionally, no. So what do you do, DJ?"

"Oh. Uh, nope, I actually work for a tech company managing their branding, but I get that question a lot. It's a missed opportunity, if you ask me."

It takes me far too long to understand his joke, but eventually I catch on. He's teasing me as if I've just asked if he deejays for a living. Because of his name. "Oh. Ha. Ha." I give a dry laugh. "How clever. You clearly missed your calling to be in comedy if you ask me."

He winks. "Or proctology. No, only kidding. But yes, I work in branding, which is fun. You know, never the same day twice and all that jazz." He waves his hand away, as if it's more boring than me telling him about life working in a coffee shop. "What about you? You said you work at a restaurant, right?"

"Coffee shop," I correct him, though to be fair, that was one of the first things I told him, so he gets points for remembering anything in the ballpark. "It's fun enough."

"What do you actually want to do, though?"

"I don't know," I admit, my cheeks hot with awkward embarrassment. I've had this conversation one too many times, and it rarely ends well. "I know that sounds awful. I feel like everyone has some grand plan or dream for their life, and I think all of my life I've been waiting for that to come up for me. You know? For me to do something or try something new and have that little lightbulb go off, right? Like, 'Ah, this is what I'm supposed to do with my life.' And I have things I like to do, sure, but nothing that could be a real career. Like, I like animals, but I have no desire to become a vet or do anything medical with them. And I like music, but I'm not musically talented. I just feel…" I stop myself, realizing I'm rambling, but before I can change the subject, he nods, surprising me as he fills in my sentence.

"Like you're not actually destined to do anything?"

I nod sheepishly. This is usually the part where they tell me I should keep trying new things, that I haven't lived enough yet to know what I want, or that I should try temping at a few different jobs, or—my personal favorite—that it's lazy not to at least try to find something I feel passionate about. "Saying it out loud sounds so stupid. I'm not, like, hard on myself about it. I'm happy, really. I guess I'm just not one of those people who has to have some big dream, you know?"

"I do know," he admits, running a hand through his hair. "Actually, it's kind of refreshing to hear someone else admit that. Branding isn't exactly a dream job for me, but it's…fine. I don't have big plans for my life either, but I'm happy, you know? One day at a time. Whatever happens, happens."

"Exactly." I flop a hand in his direction. "Yes, that's exactly it."

He smiles, leaning in farther, and his eyes dart back

and forth between mine like he's planning to say something but can't decide if he can. Finally, his mouth drops open. "I know I'm supposed to wait until the end of the date to say this or, like, play really cool and wait a few days or whatever, but...I'm having a really nice time with you, Sophie." He slides his hand across the table to take mine, and my stomach flips, cheeks heating. "I'd like to see you again."

I open my mouth to respond, but he cuts me off. "You don't have to answer right now. In fact, don't. Don't answer until we're apart, that way I don't feel like I pressured you or whatever, but just...know that the offer is there, and the ball is in your court, and next time, I swear I won't be late."

I squint my eyes, feeling as if I've slipped into a dream. *Maybe that's what happened. Maybe I fell asleep waiting for him at the restaurant. Maybe I'm there right now, drooling all over the table.*

He squeezes my hand gently, snapping me back to reality, then pulls back as our waitress delivers us new drinks. When he winks at me, warmth crawls across every inch of my skin.

He's too good to be true. Jaz's voice rings in my ears, but I shut her up and shove her away. No one will ever be her, but I have to accept that and move on. She doesn't get to ruin this for me.

CHAPTER TWENTY

5—2:13:04

The house is exactly like we left it, and walking inside drains whatever wave of determination I felt moments ago. Instead, this only feels like accepting defeat. When we walked out that door hours ago, I thought I'd never have to see the inside of this house again, thought I'd never look at that awful white kitchen tile or the beige couch again.

And yet, here we are.

Though it seemed like the best plan at the time, I'm so angry at Elliot for suggesting we turn back, so angry at myself for agreeing to it. We should've taken our chances with the woods. We should've walked until we found a place that wasn't being guarded and tried to climb the fence and dealt with whatever awful results the barbed wire would've inflicted. Anything would be better than this.

Inside, the man stands in front of us both. "Open."

"Excuse me?" I ask.

He taps my chin, pulling it down and looking inside my mouth. "Lift your tongue."

Slowly, I do as he says. Satisfied, he checks my pockets next, not being shy in the way he touches me. His hands are forceful as they dig into the depths of my pockets. He runs his hands down my legs like a TSA agent and squats at my feet, tugging off my shoes and checking them, then doing the same to my socks. "Where is the key?" he demands.

"We told you we never had a key," Elliot barks.

As the man stands, his eyes flick to my chest, and my ears are suddenly on fire. I know what's coming before he says the words.

"Take off your shirt," he demands. "Bra too."

"I don't have the key!" I tell him quickly. "I swear I don't."

"Does he? Tell me if he does, and you can skip all of this."

I don't hesitate to lie. "I don't know what you're talking about. We don't have a key. The door was unlocked."

The man stays steady and silent for several seconds, perhaps waiting for me to say more like you're supposed to when you're met with silence in an interrogation. I've watched too many crime shows to be that stupid, so I say nothing. I meet his silence with some of my own.

Finally, he speaks. "Shirt. Off."

I pull my shirt out away from my chest, fanning my bra out but not removing it. A beat passes and then he bends down, pulling my shirt and bra away farther so he can get an eyeful. He spends longer looking than is necessary, and when I turn my head, Elliot meets my eyes with fury practically radiating off of him.

"Alright, enough," he cries. "You've seen she doesn't have anything."

The man stands up slowly, turning his attention to Elliot. "Your turn." With absolute precision, he repeats the process with Elliot, searching every crevice of his body until he's satisfied that neither of us have the key.

I'm not sure what Elliot did with it, but the second I met his eyes during the search of my shirt, I knew he didn't have it anymore. There's no way he would've stood for that if he could've stopped it. I'm assuming he threw it out while we were driving. With a huff and a warning that *if you break out again, I'll shoot first and ask questions never*, he leaves.

"Where is the key?" I ask Elliot the second we're alone. "Did you lose it? Or throw it out in the woods?"

His lips curl into a wicked smile, and he lowers his voice to a near whisper. "I left it under their bed."

"Robert and Nick?" My heart twinges with betraying hope. "Do you think they'll find it?"

"I don't know," he admits, crossing the room to the cabinet and taking out two glasses, which he fills with ice water. The sink is beginning to get crowded with dirty glasses that we'll eventually have to wash if we stay here much longer. "I don't even know if the same key will work for their house. There were a lot of keys on that key ring. I only had time to think quickly once we'd been found, so I have no idea if it'll work." He passes one of the glasses to me and makes his way into the living room, sitting down on the couch.

I follow his lead, sitting down on the opposite end and crossing one leg over the other before gulping down the water. I hadn't realized how thirsty I am until now. My entire body is so hot, exhausted, and starving I don't know that I'll ever leave the couch again.

"Why do you think we're here?" Elliot asks. "Why do you think Robert and Nick are here, for that matter?"

"You mean, do I think it's random? How they choose us?"

He rubs his lips together in thought, staring at his water. "I mean why us, specifically. And what are they doing with us? They have these two houses, maybe more, built out here on acres and acres of land, and they lock us up, but in all reality, they're taking care of us. Feeding us, not hurting us. Why? Why would they do that?" He shakes his head, lifting his eyes finally to find mine. "And why would they put the two of us together? And Robert and Nick together. Families."

Families. The word is heavy in my chest. "Are we a family?" I ask, knowing what he means, but still thinking it's a strange sentiment. At one point, maybe I would've considered Elliot my family, but I haven't seen him in years.

Who would even know about our connection? And why would they bring us back together? Why would they want people with others who care about them if they're planning to hurt us? Maybe we have this all wrong somehow, but I can't work it out in my head how it would be possible.

His lips part slightly, his eyes locked on mine. Finally, he releases a breath and looks away. "You were the closest thing I had to a family for a long time."

I swallow. "Me too." I hate admitting it, even now. It feels selfish, knowing I have a family that feels less like a family than this near-stranger sitting across from me. Some people would kill for what I have, a family that has never physically hurt me. A family I can still call when I want or need to. A family I get to spend holidays with on occasion. It's more than so many people have, but it doesn't feel like enough. I want a family that feels like they would choose me if they had a chance, but I've never had that, which is why I'm so loyal to the people in my life. The ones who actually *do* choose me.

It's why losing Elliot was so devastating when I'd been sure he was the endgame for me. I thought he'd chosen me for life; instead, I learned that I'd always been a choice for him, and he suddenly wanted to make a different one.

"I'm sorry I left you," he says, his voice low, not looking at me. "I was young and stupid."

"We don't have to do this…"

He looks up at me finally, his expression pinched. "I need to say this to you, Sophie. I need to say that I'm sorry and that I've regretted walking away from you that night so many times. I've thought about calling you. I've looked you up so often, started to type out messages, to try to find the right words to tell you how sorry I was, but…you seemed happy. I was young and scared, and things felt like they were moving so fast with us. We were just kids, and suddenly life felt heavy, you know? Like we'd been together so long, and the next logical step was for us to move in together, and then marriage, and it all just felt…fast. Most of my friends didn't even have serious girlfriends. Everyone told me I was missing out on the college experience, and I ignored them because I loved you." He pauses. "But then college was over, and I…I guess I resented you a little bit. And I wondered 'what if,' and it killed me. I couldn't stick around and let myself hate you or treat you badly. So I walked away because I thought it was the right thing to do, but I've spent so much time wondering. That's what no one tells you—that no matter which path you take, you'll always wonder if it was right. Or at least, I do."

Tears sting my eyes. They're the words I've needed to hear for so long. Not only an apology, but an explanation. I swallow, afraid that if I blink, I'll encourage the tears to fall. "Well, thank you. Truly, it's okay. We've both moved on."

"Have you?" he asks.

I nod, twisting my lips. "I think so. I won't lie and say it hasn't been hard or that I don't still think about you. I went through a really rough time after you left, but my friends got me out of it. I'm good now."

With a small smirk, his eyes travel the room. "Present circumstances excluded."

A laugh bubbles out of me. "Fair enough."

"We're going to get out of here," he promises me. "And when we do, I hope we can be friends again."

"I'd really like that."

His expression warms, and he nods. "Where are you staying now?"

"At the present moment?" I look around. "I'm not totally sure."

It's his turn to laugh now. "Fair enough," he repeats. I set down my glass, and he holds out his arm, surprising me, but the gesture is sweet and, if I'm being honest, exactly what I need. Eventually, I slide up against him, resting my head on his chest. He kisses my temple, and electricity races from that spot down to my toes. It feels so normal with him, even after all this time. I inhale his scent in the most non-creepy way possible, and it takes me back to a simpler time when it was just the two of us against the world.

He was supposed to be my future, and just when I

was starting to wonder if I had any sort of future at all to look forward to, he's back again.

That has to mean something, doesn't it? He runs his hand through my hair slowly. It's been a while since I felt this safe, and I have no idea how long it's going to last, but I'm going to savor it while it does. I close my eyes, listening to the steady thrum of his heartbeat.

We need a plan, but right now, rest calls to me, and for once, I'm happy to meet it.

CHAPTER TWENTY-ONE

5—2:08:22

I'm in that peaceful place between awake and asleep, where dreams still feel real, but you know you're not quite sleeping anymore, when a sound draws my attention.

I open my eyes, realizing I'm still tucked peacefully against Elliot's side, and he's sleeping at an awkward angle, his head resting in the crook of the couch to keep from moving me.

I don't have time to dwell on how sweet that might be because I hear the sound again. I glance at the countdown clock on the wall, which reads

5—2:08:22

I have no idea if it's time for our meal to be delivered, but for the first time, I feel ready to eat whatever he brings me.

Elliot stirs next to me, and I shove his chest.

"Get up," I whisper-shout, standing and brushing off my shirt as if I'm a teenager who's been caught alone with a boy for the first time. I make space between us, moving toward the opposite side of the room.

When the door opens, there's a long pause before the man sticks his head inside. Except that when he does, it's not the usual man at all. This one is taller, with thicker arms and shoulders than the previous guy. He's also not wearing a covering over his eyes. Instead, he stares directly at us, and we get a clear look at him. He has dark skin and warm, brown eyes as he studies me. His eyes flick over me just once before he shuts the door.

"Who are you?" Elliot asks, stepping forward.

The man stares back at us, but he doesn't answer straight away. He's carrying a different box this time, one that's longer and narrower.

Instead of placing it on the counter, he carries it to the living room and places it on the coffee table.

"What is this?" I ask, gesturing toward the box as he steps back.

"Sit," he says, opening the lid of the box slightly and retrieving a notebook from inside it before securing the lid back on.

I don't move. "Why?"

"Sit," he says again, gesturing toward the couch.

Elliot looks at me strangely, obviously wondering if

we should listen, but eventually we make our way around to the couch and take a seat.

"For every answer you give, you'll be given something out of this box." His voice is deep but soft somehow. Gentler than the first man. I don't know if that should put me at ease or scare me worse. I know the stories about being kidnapped. Being allowed to see the kidnappers' faces—even just their eyes—is not a good sign.

"Are they things we'll want?" Elliot asks.

"Guess we'll find out," the man says with a sigh. He opens his notebook. "For every answer you refuse to give, you'll be punished."

"Punished?" I ask, running my hands over my arms to calm the goose bumps that line them.

He doesn't look at me or respond, instead staring down at the page in front of him. "How do the two of you know each other?"

"I think you already know that." My voice is dry and brittle. Whatever this is, I already hate it.

He quirks a brow to look up at me. "Are you refusing to answer?"

"We were friends growing up," Elliot says. "And we dated for a while in high school and college."

Staring at the paper, the man jots something down and moves on. "How did you break up?"

Elliot looks down. "I broke up with her."

"Why?" the man asks with no emotion in his voice.

147

"Because I wanted to live a little before we settled down. Everyone told me I should."

The man is silent for a long time, his pen scratching across the paper. "Sophie, was Elliot your first sexual partner?"

My body boils at the question, and I look down. I'm terrified to learn what the punishment is for refusing to answer, but this feels inhumane. Still, I croak out an answer. "Yes."

"Elliot, was Sophie yours?"

He hesitates, keeping his eyes trained straight ahead. "She was the first person I slept with, yes."

Intrigued, the man looks up. "But not your first sexual experience?"

He runs a hand over his mouth. "I'd had some experience before her."

This is news to me, and the betrayal stings. We were so young when we started dating, and we'd always said we were each other's firsts. I didn't realize we needed to be so specific about everything.

The man nods, writing something down again. He looks up. "Sophie, have you ever tried to kill yourself?"

My body goes intensely cold, and it's as if the room is closing in on me, my head heavy and packed with clouds. I stare down at the scars on my wrists. I feel as though I've been stripped naked in the center of the room. Honestly, that might be preferable. "How dare you?" I ask, my teeth gritted together.

"I'm sorry, is that a refusal?" the man asks.

"I'm done playing whatever game this is." I stand up, moving toward the hall on my way to the bedroom, but he grabs my arm quickly, jerking me backward.

"I have to do this." His voice is so low of a whisper I nearly don't hear it.

"What?"

He pushes me back onto the couch, towering over me, and my throat constricts. His eyes flick toward Elliot. "Go into the kitchen and bring back a pair of scissors from the drawer beside the stove."

"What? Why?" He remains planted in his spot.

"Do it, or this will all be so much worse." The man is looking at me as he says it, and I swear I catch a hint of regret in his eyes. *He doesn't want to do this, but someone is making him.*

Slowly, Elliot stands and makes his way into the kitchen. His body is stiff as a board as he moves. I stare at the man, silently begging him to help me, to stop this, as I hear the drawer open. Moments later, Elliot reappears with a pair of green scissors.

The man grabs my hand, pulling me into a sitting position. "Cut her hair."

I swallow. I've spent years growing my hair out after a bad haircut. It feels silly, but my hair is a part of me. Cutting it off against my will is such a violation.

"I can't do that." Elliot holds the scissors close to his chest.

"Fine. Then cut her clothes completely off her

body," the man says, his tone pointed. "And we won't be replacing them."

I swallow, my body going numb. "It's okay, Elliot," I tell him. Could we take this man? Maybe. But is it worth the risk? I don't think so. I hold my hair out to him. "It's hair. It'll grow back." My voice is shaking, my eyes burning with tears, but I do my best to hide both.

Cautiously, Elliot lowers the scissors to my shoulders, sliding hair between the blades.

"Shorter," the man says. "Chop it all off."

I close my eyes, letting the first tears fall, but Elliot pulls the scissors back. "Please. There has to be something else we can do."

"I told you the other option. Remove her clothes so she has nothing to wear or chop off all of her hair."

The sentence feels like a nursery rhyme that is so out of place here it makes me sick. Fuming, I grab the scissors from Elliot and suck in a deep breath, chopping off my own hair so no one can do it to me. If it's going to be done, I'd rather it be by me. I lop it off in sections until it's just an inch or two long all around. I imagine I look something like Angelica's Cynthia doll on *Rugrats*.

The man holds his hand out for the scissors, and I consider stabbing them through his palm, but I place them there instead with no desire to find out what the next punishment will be.

He steps backward, checking his notes again. "Now, same question."

I have nothing left to give, no fight left in me. "Yes, once."

"When?"

"After Elliot broke up with me." I can't bear to look either one of them in the eye. "It was dumb. I was devastated, and I thought it would bring him back to me. Instead"—I pause, looking away—"instead, I met my best friend. She was visiting her grandma in the hospital at the time, and our rooms were near each other's. She accidentally walked into my room once and…she saved my life."

Elliot's eyes are drilling into me, and I can feel his shock over this revelation, but he doesn't say anything.

"Next question," I demand.

"Next one is for Elliot." He looks up. "Who is the first person you had sexual intercourse with after your break-up with Sophie?"

He's silent for a long time. So long that I'm not sure he's even heard the question. "I don't remember. It's been a long time. Probably someone random."

"Are you sure about that?"

My chest expands with a deep inhale.

Elliot buries his face in his hands. "Why are you doing this?"

"I just need an answer."

"It was Caroline, okay?" He's looking at me now. "I'm sorry, Soph. It was once. We ran into each other at a bar, and it just…happened. It didn't mean anything, and it was after we broke up."

My body feels like it's working of its own accord as I turn to face him, practically pulsing red. "My sister-in-law?"

He drops his head, staring at his hands. "It is my biggest regret. I swear to you, I hate myself for it. I loved you. I never wanted to hurt you. I was lost after I left, and I made some shitty choices, but that is by far the worst."

I run through what he's telling me in my head, still waiting for him to admit it's clearly a joke and he'd never actually do that. Then it hits me. My first niece was born around a year after Elliot and I broke up. Caroline married my brother shortly after she found out she was pregnant, though they'd been dating for years before that.

"Are you Charlotte's father?"

He scowls. "What? No. Of course not."

"Are you sure?"

He opens his mouth, then closes it again. "It was a mistake, Soph. A one-time thing because she was fighting with your brother, and we were both drunk and stupid. You have to believe me." He reaches out his hand for mine, but I jerk it away.

"Don't touch me."

"Sophie, the last question is for you, and then we're done, okay?" the man asks, his voice softer than before. "Was Elliot the love of your life?"

I have to process the question. After the revelation we just discovered, I want to say I never loved him at all. That what we had meant nothing, but realistically, I know I can't do that. It would be a lie.

The truth is, I loved Elliot with everything in me for most of my life, before and after the break-up. He has always felt like the one who got away, and there was a time when I might've said he was the love of my life.

But...

"No."

If I really think about it, I was happy with Elliot, yes. But we were kids. We didn't have any grasp on the realities of life. We were nothing but passion and hormones, and looking back, that entire relationship feels more like a fever dream than true love.

I'm not even sure I can blame him for what he did with Caroline, as much as it stings. It's more a betrayal to my brother than me. We were broken up, and he had every right to do what he wanted. He doesn't owe me anything now, and he didn't owe me anything back then.

We are two strangers who used to care about each other. That's it. I have to remember that.

"He wasn't. I loved him, I think. But I've experienced all-consuming love, and it wasn't with Elliot."

The man jots one last thing down in his notebook and snaps it closed. "Well done. You can open the box now."

"What's in it?" I peer at it cautiously.

"Open it and find out."

Neither of us move as the man watches us. Eventually, he nods, then he eases back toward the door, shutting and locking it behind him. For half a second earlier, I'd hoped the door opening would be Nick and Robert, coming to apologize, but now I have no idea what to make of this second man or what just happened.

He has to be working with the first man—they were wearing similar protective suits, minus the face covering, but we've certainly never been quizzed like that.

With the door closed, I turn toward Elliot and the box. He's staring down into it with a strange expression, one that mimics the confusion I feel.

"I'm so sorry, Soph." He looks to be on the verge of tears, but I wave him off.

"It was a long time ago. It doesn't matter anymore."

"Of course it matters." He takes hold of my hand, looking down at my wrist. Slowly, he lifts it to his lips and presses a kiss to my scar. "If I'd known…"

I pull my wrist back. "You'd what? Have stopped having sex with my sister-in-law long enough to come check on me?"

He winces. "I deserve that."

"You think?" I sigh, rubbing my hand over my forehead. "Look, none of that matters anymore. We've both moved on. Right now, we need to focus on figuring out how to get out of here." *So I never have to see you again.*

I can tell he wants to argue by the way he's pinning me with a hard stare, but eventually, he nods. "If that's what you want."

"It is."

I turn toward the box. "What do you think? Should we open it?"

Slowly, he lifts the lid, peeking inside like there might be a snake waiting for him.

"It looks like...things to do. Games, books, snacks." He pulls the lid the rest of the way off, revealing a chessboard and a game of Clue, then two crossword puzzles, and a mystery novel. Next is a bag of cheesy popcorn and a package of chocolate chip cookies. He reaches his hand in for whatever is next but stops, pulling his hand back so I can get a look at what it is that has him frozen in place.

"A knife," I say quietly. A much larger knife than the one left in the drawers for us. It doesn't mean anything. Perhaps it's a matching one for the kitchen set, and they're simply returning it to us. It doesn't make any sense, but I cross the room to check the drawers in the kitchen, just in case, and my jaw drops.

Everything has been replaced with plastic cutlery, but when did they do that? I haven't used silverware since the day I tried to stab the man. I run my hand through the drawer of plastic utensils in total disbelief.

The longer I'm here, the more and more this place feels like a simulation. I lift my hand to my fresh haircut. Some things feel all too real, though.

"What are you doing?" Elliot asks, studying me from across the room with a wary expression.

"That's the only weapon in the house now," I say.

"There were knives before, but…" I trail off. "Why would they give us that?" My stomach feels like it's full of rocks.

He reaches into the box and pulls out the only other thing left: a bottle of pills. "I don't know. Why would they give us these?" Spinning it around, I check again to be sure the bottle doesn't have a label to tell us what the pills are. Carefully, he places both the knife and the pills on the table next to the snacks and activities and crosses his arms, clearly as puzzled as I feel.

"I don't understand," I whisper. "What the hell is this supposed to be?"

He drops down onto the couch, his elbows resting on his knees. "I have no idea. Should we pack it all back up?"

"No. The knife will help," I say. "It's something for protection if nothing else."

He nods. "Right. Okay."

I pick up the pill bottle, turning it around in my palm. The pills are green and oblong, but there's nothing distinguishable about them. Something about them is familiar to me, though, and the longer I stare at them, the more certain I am that I've seen them some-where before.

CHAPTER TWENTY-TWO

BEFORE — FIVE DAYS AGO

"You're early," I say as I walk into the restaurant where we agreed to meet and spot DJ already at a table.

He stands up, pulling me in for a hug and kissing my head. "Have you met me? I'm incredibly punctual." He winks and waits for me to sit down before taking the seat across from me. "I came straight from work. I wasn't going to chance anything happening this time."

I'm touched by the gesture since it means he's been here for something like an hour already. "You didn't have to do that."

"I wanted to make it up to you," he admits, looking sheepish. "I ordered you a Manhattan with extra cherries." He nudges the drink toward me. "That's your drink, right?"

I nod, staring down at it with a strange pit in the center of my chest. It's kind of him to have ordered my drink, so I should probably just drink it, but then again,

I know I can't. I also know telling him this could potentially ruin this date, if not worse. Women have been killed over denying drinks, and I'm incredibly aware of this as I stare at the brown liquid in the tumbler in front of me.

DJ has been nothing but a gentleman to me, and I should trust him. I hate that I can't. I hate that this is the world we live in. I'm overreacting, I know, and I'm going to offend him, but eventually I fold my hands together.

"Thank you for this. It's so sweet, but I'm actually not drinking tonight."

"Oh." His face falls, and I hold my breath, but he recovers quickly. I had nothing to worry about, and I should've known. "Okay, no problem. Sorry, I shouldn't have assumed."

"No, I'm sorry," I say quickly. "Really. It was so sweet that you remembered—"

"Not a big deal," he says, waving his hand through the air as if he's dusting the drink and the issue off the table. "Is everything okay?"

"Totally," I assure him, now a bit disappointed that I won't be able to drink. "I just have an early morning tomorrow, and I don't want to have a headache." I sigh. "The joys of inching closer to thirty, am I right?"

He presses his lips together with a playful grin. "Tell me about it. We're basically decrepit." His hand goes into the air to wave our waiter over, and I ask for an Arnold Palmer before we order our dinner.

When we're alone again, he folds his hands under his chin and beams at me. "So how was your day?"

"Oh, it was fine. I worked until two, and then Jaz and I went to her grandma's to help her sort through her attic because she's getting ready to move into an assisted living facility."

"Oh." He tilts his head to the side. "That's sad."

"It is," I admit with a sigh. "Jaz is trying to be tough because that's just how she is, but it's hard on her whole family."

"Are they close?"

"She's super close with her grandma, yeah. And her parents and siblings are relatively close, too."

"That must be nice," he says, and I catch a hint of something sad and bitter in his tone, but we're interrupted by the waiter bringing my drink to the table, so I have to wait to be able to ask him to elaborate.

"You aren't close with your family?"

He puts down his drink and wipes his mouth. "It's nothing serious. We were just never really close. It sounds cliché and melodramatic to say they never understood me, but I guess that's the best explanation. What about you? Are you close with your family?"

I shake my head. "Not particularly, no."

"It's probably shitty to say it's nice to not be alone in that," he says with a dry chuckle, rubbing the back of his neck before meeting my eyes.

"It's not," I assure him. "It's honest."

"Maybe a little too honest."

I reach across the table without meaning to, cupping my hand over the back of his. "Sometimes it's tough having my best friend have a perfect family. Maybe 'perfect' isn't the right word, but a family who loves each other unconditionally. Who calls to check in. Who celebrates her wins. I love it for her, but that doesn't mean I don't get jealous. It's easy to think everyone has a family like that, so it's always a nice reminder that there are more people out there like us than we think."

His expression warms slowly, like a thawing glacier, and eventually he turns his hand over and holds mine. "Where did you come from?"

"Heaven, obviously," I tease.

He laughs. "Seriously, how is it possible you're still single? What guy do I need to thank for screwing this up so perfectly for me?"

I take a sip of my drink, buying myself time. "I've never been a big dater, to be honest. I had one serious relationship through most of college, and then afterward Jaz and I dated for a while, but that didn't work 'cause we were better off as friends, so here I am." A nervous giggle bubbles out of me. I haven't mentioned to him that I previously dated my best friend-slash-roommate, though I have pansexual as my orientation on the app, so I'm assuming it won't be too big of an issue. Still, that doesn't stop the moment from being filled with a bit of anxiety every time I have to tell someone new.

Honestly, in the year of our Lord 2024, how is this even still an issue?

"Lucky me," he says with a small smile. "Remind me to thank Jaz when I meet her."

"When?" I tease. "Someone's cocky."

He squeezes my hand. "I prefer confident." Then he changes the subject back to awkward territory. "Do you mind me asking what happened with the guy in college? You know, so I can make notes of what not to do."

Another sip of my drink. Another awkward pause. Then I say, "We just grew apart, I guess. We were really serious for a while."

"Like thinking-of-marriage serious?" he asks.

Slowly, regretfully, I nod. "I thought so, anyway. But then he started pulling away. And then one day, he just said he needed some space. He said it was a break, but I never heard from him again." I shrug one shoulder, trying to seem more unbothered than I feel. "And that was that."

"I'm sorry." His thumb strokes over the soft skin of my palm.

"No, it's fine, honestly. It was a long time ago."

We're interrupted as the waitress arrives with our food, setting the plates down in front of us. I unroll my silverware and place the cloth napkin on my lap before asking, "What about you? Why are *you* still single? Is it because of your horrible personality?" I wrinkle my nose, mocking him, and he narrows his eyes at me playfully.

He sighs, resting his arms against the table. "I was with a girl a few years ago who really messed me up, to be totally real with you. She was emotionally abusive to the point that I had severe self-esteem issues after we broke up. It's taken me quite a while and a lot of therapy to get to a good place again."

"Wow." It's so hard for me to believe this man could ever have self-esteem issues, but the hard reality is that none of us is ever allowed to believe we're perfect, even if we look it on the outside. "I'm really sorry. Therapy has been really important to me, too. I'm such an advocate for it now."

He shrugs, cutting into his steak. "Same, but, well, I guess I should thank her. Without that mess, we might not be here tonight. If I hadn't gone through all of that, I might not have met you. And *that* would be a tragedy."

"Fair enough," I say, breathless at the compliment.

"Actually, we should toast to them. For breaking our hearts and leading us here." He holds up his drink, clearly waiting for me to join him in this ridiculous toast. When I do, he grins broadly. "To Briana Loverling."

"And Elliot Galitzine." I tap my drink against his as his eyes twinkle, and we both say goodbye to our pasts and hello to whatever the future might bring.

CHAPTER TWENTY-THREE

5—1:23:56

Eventually, we open the bags of snacks and munch on them cautiously. Since they were sealed, I'm assuming they're as safe as the other chips were. I'm also nearly too hungry and emotionally exhausted to care.

The pills are still bothering me, but I can't quite put my finger on where I've seen them before.

Elliot picks up one of the crossword puzzle books and digs a pencil out of the bottom of the box. "Well, I guess this gives us one clue. Clearly, whoever this is, they don't know you very well."

"What do you mean?" I ask, popping another piece of popcorn into my mouth.

"You hate crossword puzzles. If whoever brought us here knew you at all, they'd know that."

I raise my eyebrows. He's not wrong, but it's also the last thing on my mind. "Well, maybe I don't hate them now. You don't know me anymore, Elliot. I think that game proves how little we ever really knew each other." It's an unnecessary jab, but I'm still not over everything I just found out, even if I'm trying desperately to pretend I am.

"Maybe so," he says plainly. "But I refuse to believe you've changed that much. Feel free to prove me wrong." He holds the book out, waiting to see if I'll take it. We both know I won't.

I shake my head. "Fine. Whatever. They got the crossword puzzle thing wrong, but they did bring some of my favorite snacks." I lift up the bag of popcorn.

"Okay, fine, but that's easy enough. Who doesn't love popcorn and chocolate chip cookies? It's like America's two favorite snacks. It could be a lucky guess. Or if they do know you, it could be someone who knew you on a very basic level. Someone who has seen you at a vending machine, maybe. Or someone you went to the movies with."

I drop another handful of popcorn into my mouth before leaning forward to pick up the pills. My body has never been so grateful for food. I'm inhaling it as if it were air. There's no way these two snacks will last us until tomorrow, so I should really pace myself, but I won't. I can't.

I shake the pills, turning them over in my hand.

"Speaking of going to the movies...um"—he clears his throat, leaning forward—"have you? I mean, have you been seeing anyone? I know you said you weren't dating seriously, but have you been dating even casually?"

I shake my head, starting to say that it's none of his business, but my voice catches because I suddenly think that might be a lie. Now, with these pills in my hand and that question in my mind, something has clicked deep inside my skull.

A face, though it's hidden behind the thick fog that has encompassed my mind since our arrival. A name. A voice.

"Sophie?" he asks, trying to draw me out of my trance, but I'm deep inside my head, searching and clawing for answers.

"There were pills on his counter," I whisper, sudden tears filling my eyes and spilling over without warning.

"What are you—"

"Pills." I shake the bottle at him. "These pills." Slowly, I run a hand over my face to dry my cheeks. "The guy I was dating, he, um, he had these pills on his counter in the kitchen. I'm remembering it. Him."

He's serious all of a sudden, sitting up straight, hands resting on his knees. "You are? Who was it? What do you remember? Do you think it was the man who brought us here?"

"I don't…" I'm trying so hard to remember, but it's that familiar feeling of trying to pull a dream back from the depths of your subconscious as it quickly fades away. Attempting to catch smoke in my palm as it slips between my fingers. "I don't know. I don't

165

remember. We hadn't been dating for long, I don't think. But..." But had we? How much of my memory is missing? What if it's entire months? Years, even? How would I know? My throat is tight. I can't breathe.

"But what?" he demands.

"But..." I look at the pills again. "I mean, he has to be, doesn't he? What are the odds?"

"You need to think," he says seriously, his face calm and solemn. "You need to think hard. Remember. If the pills are what got you there, maybe something else in this box will help, too. Maybe something else in here..." He begins pulling things out of the pile and tossing them at me, begging for more of the memory to resurface.

"I can't. I'm sorry. I'm trying." I shove everything off of my lap and stand up, fingers pressed into my temples.

"Where are you going?" he cries, following me as I rush down the hallway.

"I just need a minute," I say, waving a hand at him to get him to stay away from me. I'm suffocating, the walls are closing in, and being close to him, under the weight of his expectations, is only making it worse. "Please give me a minute."

I don't look back to make sure he's listening, just slam the bathroom door and sink down against the floor, sobs spilling over and escaping my chest. The sound of his footsteps retreating brings me little peace, and now I don't know if I actually wanted him to give me the space I asked for or if I just wanted him to prove he's going to do better and actually be here for me when I need him.

My body is shaking before I realize it's happening. Nothing about this new reality feels real. Are the memories I'm having—of the date I can't quite remember—even true? Could they be fabrications of my mind? Could I just be looking for pieces to connect when they don't exist?

I just want answers, but they aren't anywhere to be found.

Right now, my only clue—real or imagined—is the bottle of pills and the fact that whoever brought me here had to have known about my relationship with Elliot. Aside from random people we went to college with, the only people currently in my life who would connect Elliot to me or have any idea how to contact him when even I couldn't be sure how to do that are my family and Jaz.

Jaz isn't a suspect in the slightest. She would never hurt me. Never leave me.

Except…she did.

She left me in one way in order to hold on to me in another. And for that, I could never hate her.

I force that thought away. I don't have time for that spiral right now. There's too much at stake. I need to put the pieces of this puzzle together, though Elliot's right; puzzles of any kind have never been my favorite thing.

The bottom line is that no one is coming to save me, and if I want to make it out of this place, I need to be smart. Strategic. I need to get myself out of here. Home.

The thought crosses my mind, and I hate it, but I have to consider it: is this some weird conversion therapy of some kind? Could my parents have had me locked up with Elliot in hopes that I'd magically come out straight? They never loved the idea that I'm not their picture-perfect child like my brother and sister-in-law, or that I may never have biological children, though my brother is certainly taking care of the grandchild quota with his litter. But I can't imagine they'd do anything this cruel. Or that they'd care enough to be bothered with it.

It would be unforgivable. They have to know that.

They couldn't truly be okay with me never speaking to them again, could they? I think back to what the man first said to me when I arrived.

I'm here to help you.

I hadn't thought much about it with everything else going on, but what else could he have meant? Help me how? I go to therapy for my mental health. I've been okay. I don't need help there, so what else could it be?

I'm not in a perfect place in life, maybe, but who in their twenties could honestly say they are? I'm making it through the days and figuring out who I am the best I can.

Before I've had time to process it completely, the

bathroom is plunged into complete darkness. I squeal and push up on my feet, looking around. "What the hell?"

"Are you okay?" Elliot calls from the living room or kitchen—far enough away that his voice sounds softer than normal. The only light in the room is coming from under the door, which means the entire house's power isn't out, only this room.

I wrap my hand around the doorknob, preparing to open it, but suddenly hear a clicking sound. Like someone is typing something. Then, a red light reflects on the wall. I turn back around to stare at the space on the wall where I know the mirror is, and a shard of ice lodges itself in my throat.

On the mirror, there are two words typed in red, digital font.

HELLO, SOPHIE.

I put a hand to my chest, gasping for breath. *Is this really happening?* Instantly, the words disappear and are quickly replaced with new ones.

DON'T SCREAM. I WANT TO HELP YOU.

That message again. Is it possible they read my thoughts earlier?

I CAN GET YOU OUT OF HERE.

I keep both hands on the doorknob, ready to bolt but refusing to move. *What is happening? I'm dreaming. I have to be dreaming. This has to be a dream. Things like this don't happen in real life.*

> BUT IN ORDER TO DO THAT, I NEED
> SOMETHING FROM YOU.

I want to cry out, to demand for this person to tell me who they are, but I don't want Elliot to hear. Then again, maybe I should tell him to come see this for himself. He's never going to believe me if I don't.

I twist the doorknob, opening my mouth to call for him, and the words disappear. There is more typing as I wait for the next message to appear. When it does, all at once, the words cause my knees to go weak.

> TAKE THE KNIFE AND KILL ELLIOT. ONCE
> YOU'VE DONE SO, YOU'LL BE FREE
> TO GO.

I cover my mouth, blinking and rubbing my eyes, convinced this is a dream as the words disappear once more, replaced with a final message.

> GOOD LUCK.

Then, the lights come back on.

CHAPTER TWENTY-FOUR

5—1:23:35

I stumble out of the room in a daze, tucking my shaking hands into the pockets of my jeans. There's so much to unpack already, and I don't know where to begin. Why would they ask me to kill Elliot? Could they possibly think I'd be awful enough or desperate enough to do it?

Also, the fact that whoever sent the message knew I was the one in the bathroom, or that there was someone in the bathroom in the first place, means that there are cameras in this house somewhere. The thought is chilling to somewhere deep in my core.

The room is filled with a sinister, silent air as I walk into the living room and find Elliot sitting on the couch, staring at the far wall where the countdown timer is.

He's pale and looks like he might be getting ready to vomit as his eyes find mine, and he stands. He looks sweaty and terrified, as if he's been caught doing something awful.

"Are you okay?" he asks, voice shaking. "I'm sorry I pushed you. I just…it was the first hint we'd gotten, and it…I thought it might be the way for us to get out of here."

"I know," I say simply, scanning the table. Everything looks just the way it was when I left it, which means the knife should be in the box.

Not that I'm going to pick it up. I just want to look at it, I guess. I'm not going to hurt Elliot. Obviously. It's impossible. I can't. I wouldn't. But I also know that if the person responsible for all of this is watching me, it's best to put on a show. To at least make him think I'm considering his offer.

Is any of it true? I guess that thought hadn't occurred to me. If I kill him, would they let me go? Why would they want him dead in the first place?

When I look back over at Elliot, he's staring down, somewhat out of it, and I have to wonder if he senses the shift in me. The wondering. The uncertainty and fear I'm now plagued with more than ever before.

I open my mouth to say something, anything to quell the tension that is potentially one-sided, but I'm interrupted by a sound at the door, and Elliot stands at attention.

"What's that?" he asks, looking at me.

Perhaps the first man is back to bring us our meal for the day, but I had assumed these snacks were all we'd be getting. If that isn't the case, why wouldn't the other guy have brought it all at once?

Elliot moves to stand in front of me, blocking me from whoever is coming as the door opens, and suddenly, we're staring into a familiar face that takes me a second to recognize.

"Nick?" Elliot calls first, figuring it out before I do.

Nick steps into the house slowly, eyes surveying the space. "Oh my god. I'm so glad it's you. Are you guys okay?"

"How did you find us?" I ask, moving toward the coffee table to peek into the box while Elliot is distracted.

He holds up the key proudly. "Nice job leaving this behind. How'd you know it would work for our door, too?"

"I didn't," Elliot admits. "I was hoping. Guessing, really. I thought it was better with you guys than in our place. Where's your dad?" Elliot peers his head around Nick to catch sight of Robert, but he's not there.

Nick shuts the door behind him just as I reach the box and look inside, and my heart drops. I nudge it to the side, trying to see if I was wrong about where we'd left the knife. Maybe Elliot laid it beside the box, not inside of it, but I don't see anything.

The knife is missing.

Suddenly, my mind flashes back to the moment when I walked out of the bathroom and how Elliot was staring at the wall so intently. Is it possible…

173

My insides are like sludge, like quicksand pulling me down, down, down, into the reality I'm now faced with. Did Elliot get a similar message? Did they tell him to kill me so he could leave?

If so, is he going to accept their offer?

My eyes land on Nick, who is standing with the door shut just behind him. His hand is hidden behind his back, and I thought it was because he'd just closed the door, but now I realize I've been wrong.

Slowly, he pulls his hand out, revealing a knife of his own. This one isn't ours. The handle is blue, not black, but it's similar enough.

He holds it in the air with a trembling hand. "I'm so sorry," he whispers, eyes wide and wild with a palpable sense of fear.

Elliot puts his hands up, taking a step back. "What are you doing?"

"I have to do this," he whispers. "It's the only way." He lunges for Elliot, the knife swiping through the air, and Elliot drops to the ground, reaching for something under the couch. He pulls out the knife, rolling across the floor and scooting away from Nick as he clumsily lunges for him again.

It's then that I notice the blood on the hem of Nick's blue T-shirt.

"Nick!" I shout, staring at him in horror. "What happened? What did you do?" I'm trying to draw his attention my way to buy Elliot time, but I'm also beginning to put the pieces together fully. He wouldn't have… "Please tell me you didn't…"

"Don't look at me like that. It's all your fault!" He shakes his head, lifting his hands to his temples and cupping his scalp, knife still in hand. "You fucking people. You ruined everything. We were fine. We were safe! Then you came along, and everything went to shit." He lunges at Elliot again, but Elliot pulls the door to the pantry open just in time and Nick's knife connects with it instead.

Angrily, Nick jerks it out of the wood, growling like a rabid animal.

"Did he tell you to kill us?" I ask him, my voice quivering. "Did he tell you to kill us, and you'd be set free?"

He turns to face me, face scrunched with anger or confusion—I'm not totally sure which. "What did you just say?" He points a finger at me. "What are you talking about?"

"Because that's what he told me," I admit, my heart racing in my chest so loudly they can probably hear it from across the room. "And we don't have to do any of that. You have the key. We can just go." I gesture toward the door. "All of us. We can just go. Elliot and I know the way out of here. We'll show you. We can protect each other."

Behind him, Elliot is standing up, watching the interaction with concern.

Nick's expression is conflicted—a whirlpool of

disbelief and rage. "Why would you do that? Why would you help me after what we did to you?"

"You didn't have a choice. We know that. You had to tell him where we were hiding. We don't blame you." I pause. "Or your dad."

"I didn't hurt him," Nick says, blinking his blood-shot eyes slowly. "They told us they were going to kill us both, or we could choose one of us to die and the other could go. He took the pills so I could leave. I didn't want him to. I would've never asked him to...but he did it so I could get out, then they didn't even work. The pills, they...it wasn't enough. And he took the knife." He scrubs tears off of his cheeks angrily, looking away. "He did it so I could leave, and then, after he was gone, after it was too late to take it back or undo it, we found out it didn't matter. It was all for nothing. His sacrifice wasn't enough. Not for them. Oh no, then they told me I had to do this, too."

"How do you know this will be enough either?" Elliot asks. "What if you go through with this, and they still don't let you go?"

Nick's mouth drops open like he's planning to say something, a string of spit hanging between his lips. He shakes his head slowly, his eyes haunted. "It's the only way. This. I have to do this. I don't want to. I'm not a killer, but I have kids, man." He sobs, hand still trembling as he holds the knife. "I have two kids." His hand goes down to his knees to show their height. "They need me. Their mom needs me."

"So let's go, then," I tell him. "We'll just go. We'll find a way. The three of us together. We'll get you home to your wife and kids." I hold out my hand, trying to get him to put the knife down. "You don't want to do this. They need their father, like you said. They need him to not be in prison."

"No. No, this isn't a fucking fairy tale. We aren't all walking out of here into the sunset. If we try it, he'll shoot us," he shouts. "He'll shoot us. He'll kill us. We can't leave." He lifts the knife again. "We'll never make it. This is the only way." Without warning, he lunges for me.

I scream and jerk backward, but his movements stop in an instant, his knees going forward quicker than the rest of him. He's frozen, almost comically so, and then he drops to the ground. I didn't see Elliot move, but he must've seen what was coming before I did. He had less hope than I did about being able to convince Nick to leave together.

Our knife is still in Nick's back as he drops down on all fours and falls forward, flat on his stomach, his eyes blinking slowly, breaths ragged. Tears cascade across his nose and down his temple onto the floor, and he lets out a whimper like a dog.

Elliot and I stare at each other for several seconds, neither of us blinking before he drops his gaze to Nick, still lying helpless between our feet.

"I can't believe you did that." I don't know how to feel. On one hand, he just saved our lives, but on the other, I have to think there was another way. He'd just lost his father. He was as much a victim in all of this as we are.

"I didn't think I had a choice. Are you okay?" Elliot asks, drawing my attention back to him.

I nod, putting a hand on my chest before stepping forward and kicking Nick's knife away from his hand. "What do we do?" I ask.

"We should go," Elliot says, reaching for my hand.

"We can't just leave him here."

He rushes toward me with new determination in his dark eyes. "That's exactly what we have to do. We have to leave him, and we have to go now." Without warning, he bends down, searches in Nick's pocket for the key, and once he has it, he grabs my arm, and we barrel toward the door.

He's right, and I know it. If my theory is correct, the man already knows what we've done and that we're leaving. Our only hope is out there.

CHAPTER TWENTY-FIVE

5—1:23:20

We rush down the stairs, but I stop us. "Wait!" I shout, running back inside the house.

"Where are you going?"

"I have to get the knife." He follows closely behind me as we make our way inside. I walk cautiously toward Nick's body, half expecting him to reach out suddenly and grab my ankle.

I bend down, squeeze my eyes shut, and jerk the knife out of Nick's back. It takes more effort than I expected to pull it free, and he groans as the sickening, squishing sound slices through the air.

I can't help thinking of my conversation with Jaz about the men who post photos of their latest kills on their dating profile. What would she say if she could see me now? *Would she call me a poacher, too?*

I can't look at his body anymore. He's not dead yet, and I don't know if it's better or worse that I can't put him out of his misery or go and get help. We just have to leave him and let things run their course.

I'm not sure I'll ever be able to wipe this image from my mind or this feeling from my gut.

Wincing, I dry the knife on my pants, trying not to think too hard about the action before I pick up the second knife and make my way back out the door. I pass Elliot one of the knives, refusing to second guess it, and follow him down the stairs. This time, we know which direction to head, so we make our way toward the tree line and up the overgrown path next to the fallen tree that we're both fairly certain leads toward the fence line we saw earlier.

At night, the woods are dark and eerie, filled with shadows and noises all around. I'm listening closely for the sounds of footsteps or an engine nearby, a warning that he's coming for us.

When we spot a light up ahead, we both stop almost at once. Elliot puts a hand on my shoulder, shoving me back against the tree and shielding me with his body.

We wait, both barely breathing as we watch the light for signs of movement and listen for sounds of talking.

Eventually, he turns to face me, his voice low. "We took the wrong path again."

"What? How do you know?"

"It's a house up there," he says, running a hand over his forehead. "Another house. Either we've gone the wrong way, or we overlooked this earlier."

I nod, having just worked that out, too. It's not Nick and Robert's house—it's in a different direction—but whatever light we're seeing must be a different one. Someone else that's trapped here.

Everything in the woods is so disorienting. It feels like Wonderland, everything slightly spooky and otherworldly. Nothing about this place makes sense.

"Should we go see if we can get help?" he asks.

I open my mouth. "Honestly, I don't trust anyone else. We saw how it turned out with Nick and Robert." They both betrayed us in different ways, and now they're both dead. I didn't want them to be. I only wanted us to all make it home safely. Thinking of Nick's family, the children he'll never come home to, threatens to break me, so I can't dwell on it. I can't think about anything except getting out.

"Do you trust me?" he asks, and I'm suddenly very aware of his hand on my arm, his body pressed against mine.

I give him a stiff nod. "I don't have much of a choice right now, do I?"

"Were you thinking of taking their offer?" He looks away as he asks it, like he's afraid to know the answer. I'm sort of afraid to give it for fear of hearing his.

"No," I tell him. "It wasn't an option for me."

"Why not?" he asks, voice low as his eyes come back to meet mine. "You would've gotten out of here. You don't owe me anything."

"Because I…" I choke on my words, then stop and

collect myself. "I care about you, El. I always have. I want us to get out of here together."

He swallows, looking away. "I got the same offer. On the countdown clock."

"I figured," I tell him, my hand on his arm. His eyes flick to the knife in my opposite hand. "After Nick came, I started to assume they gave the offer to all of us."

"Do you think they're serious?"

"No. Of course not. This is all some sick game. That's why Nick did what they told him to, but it still wasn't enough. There's no way they're just going to let any of us go."

He runs his tongue over his lips. "You're willing to bet your life on it?"

"I'm not going to hurt you," I say, holding out the knife. "I wouldn't have given you a knife if I thought you'd hurt me, either. Take them both if you don't believe me. I couldn't hurt you. If I did, I'd never forgive myself. I'm not that person, no matter what it would do for me."

"Okay," he says finally, then glances over his shoulder. He doesn't take the knife from me, though. Instead, he carefully tucks his knife into his back pocket. "I have a plan."

"Care to share with the class?"

"Come with me." He takes my hand and moves toward the house in the distance.

"Where are we going?"

"If this is another house, another group of people who've also been challenged with killing each other, eventually the man is going to have to come and check on them. Which means he'll have to bring the golf cart and probably some supplies. We'll keep watch until we see him, then steal the golf cart and use it to drive along the fence and look for a way out. It'll be faster than going on foot."

"Sure. If we aren't caught first."

"They know we're gone," he says simply. "You know they do. They're already looking for us."

"How do we know they don't have cameras out in the woods?"

He's quiet for a moment, then looks back over his shoulder to say, "We don't."

I swallow, forging ahead, and when the house comes into view, I stop. This house is different from the others. Smaller. It's more like a shack or a shed than a house, in fact. There's a small porch light over the front door and the windows are bare so we can see inside, though no one seems to be home.

He jogs up the stairs and walks across the small porch. Like a doe, I walk behind him, eyes and ears peeled for any sign this is a trap.

"There's a computer," he says, cupping his hands against the sides of his face and leaning against the glass of the window to get a better look. I copy his movements, and my heart seizes over the sight of it. "We can reach out to someone for help."

I'm quiet as I survey the area, looking for cameras or signs that anyone is inside. He's right, though. If we can get to that computer, or maybe even find a phone inside, we can call for help.

"I'll go in," he tells me. "You stay here and keep an eye out. If you see anyone coming, you can just hit the window to warn me and then get yourself the hell away from here."

"No way. I'm not staying out here alone," I tell him. "We'll go together."

"Go to the woods, then."

"No. That's even worse."

"We don't know that it's safe to go in there."

"It's not any safer out here."

His eyes dart back and forth between mine as if he's trying to decide if it's worth the fight. I square my shoulders, locking my jaw. He won't convince me of anything. Fighting is pointless. Instead, I dart around him and toward the door, checking over my shoulders for signs of anyone as I go.

Elliot is close behind me as we reach the door, but as I start to unlock it, I realize the keyhole is facing me. This door isn't set up like the others because it's meant to keep people out, rather than in.

Elliot pulls the key from his pocket with a look to me that says it's worth a shot. I hold my breath as he slips the key into the hole and…

It doesn't turn.

No.

We were so close.

My chest goes tight as I watch him turn it both ways, just for the key to remain still. "It doesn't fit," he whispers. "Damn it." He pulls the key back out and examines it, then looks over at the window.

"Do you think there are alarms? We could bust through the window," I suggest.

"I'm sure there are," he says with a groan. "Maybe we should just keep walking. We'll find another house and try the original plan."

"There's a computer right there," I say, gesturing toward the window where I can see the illuminated screensaver just feet away on a desk. "If we can just get in, we can send an email that will save our lives. I'm not walking away, alarm or not."

He sighs, scrubbing a hand over his face. "Alright, fine, but stand back." Without warning, he pulls his shirt over his head, then wraps the material around his wrist and knuckles.

"I don't need you to—"

Before I can finish the thought, he slams his hand through the glass, cursing under his breath as the glass shatters everywhere. It's louder than I expected, practically echoing in the woods, and we fall silent, waiting for an alarm or a shout from the man to tell us we've been caught. That this is all over. Elliot pulls his hand back, and I spot dark blood on the gray fabric.

"Are you okay?"

"I'm fine," he huffs, unwrapping his hand. "Just go.

Hurry up." He juts his head toward the window, rushing me inside. I ease myself through the window, carefully maneuvering over the broken shards of glass. A piece nicks my leg just as I make it through, and I clap my hand to the back of my thigh, limping as I hurry toward the computer and lay down my knife. I have no idea how much time we have, and I don't want to waste a single second.

Blood smears across the mouse as I wiggle it on the screen to wake the computer.

My heart sinks. "It's locked. We need the password."

Of course it's locked. Why wouldn't it be? I spin around to face Elliot, who has his hand unwrapped and is examining a gash that runs along his knuckle. He winces, pulling a shard of glass out of the cut.

I turn back to the computer. There has to be something. I know nothing about this man that would be helpful in guessing his password, but maybe...

I search beside the computer, running my hands over the desk in search of a paper with the password on it. I probably won't be that lucky, but I have to try.

I lift the keyboard, but there's nothing there.

Wait.

Something yellow catches my eye, and I turn the keyboard completely over, my body filling with butterflies at the sight of a yellow sticky note taped to the underside of the keyboard with one word written on it:

MrBigD69!

I hold in a groan, and Elliot snorts behind me as I type in the password and bite my bottom lip, waiting. Within seconds, the screen changes.

"That was it. We're in." I open the internet browser, thinking quickly, and try to go to Facebook, but my account is locked down with two-factor authentication, and having no phone, I can't access it. I go to my email next, which also requires me to approve the sign in from my mobile device.

Frustration bubbles up in my gut as I look back over my shoulder to where Elliot is carefully wrapping his hand again. In the dark, he looks extra pale, and I worry about how much blood he's losing.

"You good?"

He nods, looking at the computer. "Keep going."

I groan, returning my attention to the browser and trying to log into my email another way.

"Security question," I say with a sigh of relief. *Now if I can just remember how I answered it. Did I have capitals? Does that matter?*

I press enter and hold my breath as the screen goes white. Then…

"I'm in!"

I click the button to start my email and type in Jaz's email address, unexpected tears stinging my eyes. We're so close. We're absolutely, positively so close. I have no idea what to say or how to say it. I don't know where I am or how to tell her to find me.

I begin to type the first thing I can think of:

Don't give up on me. I'm here. Wishing to come back to you. I've been taken. Kidnapped, I guess. Locked in a house with Elliot. Some man is keeping us here...maybe someone I dated? I can't remember anything. Please just...don't give up. I miss you. I miss Simon. I love you so much, Jaz. If I never get to say that to your face again, please know I love you. If I get a second chance, I'll risk everything. Don't give up on me.

I look over at Elliot, who is tactfully giving me privacy to type my email. "Should I say anything else?"

He reads through it. "Would you mind giving her my mom's number?" He rattles it off. "Have her let her know I'm alive."

I do as he's asked me to, then press send.

"Now what?"

He nervously checks out the window. "We probably shouldn't wait around. I'm going to look and see if there's a phone hidden in here somewhere."

The one-room shack is small and there are only two desks, one with the computer and another with several water rings and a notebook on its wooden top. There are no drawers, but Elliot lies on the ground and checks under everything while I start looking behind the desks.

A noise sounds from the desktop, and I walk back to the computer, my heart racing as I open my inbox, but there's still no response. Instead, a little icon on the bottom of the screen is now flashing blue. I click on it, and the screen suddenly fills with several boxes.

Cameras.

There are dozens and dozens of video screens, all of nearly identical apartments, numbered 1-6, each with a different countdown clock on the wall.

I gasp, leaning in to get a better look. From what I can tell, there seems to be a camera in every single room, including the bathroom. There are cameras inside the showers and even inside the toilet.

I'm going to be sick. I press a hand to my stomach as I feel Elliot touch my shoulder, leaning in to see what I'm looking at.

In Robert's apartment, I see the man dressed in black standing over his body, and I force myself to look away. In another video, a woman is cradling a young girl on the couch. In yet another, there's an older couple standing in the kitchen.

"There are six houses," Elliot says softly. He scowls, his voice lowering into a whisper. "That's what the numbers mean in front of the countdowns. Each number represents a different house. We were number five, Nick and Robert were number three." He pauses, looking around the room. "What the fuck is this place?"

"I don't know," I admit, looking over the screen again. In the corner, something caught my eye that I hadn't noticed before. A single letter at the edge of the screen, almost invisible, like a watermark. But it's there. Simply: D.

D.

MrBDig69!

It didn't click for me earlier, but for some reason it does now.

I hear Jaz's voice ringing in my head, joking about something. My head is an echo chamber of her voice and another voice, one that's familiar though I can't place it, and then, like the flick of a light switch—I remember everything.

CHAPTER TWENTY-SIX

BEFORE — FIVE DAYS AGO

"I never do this," I say as DJ opens the door to his apartment. It's cliché, and it's also a pretty blatant lie, but it's not a lie that I don't typically do this on the second date at least. I'm a third-date girlie—old-fashioned values and all of that.

"Well, I'm glad to know I'm the exception." He gives me a cocky, lopsided grin before pushing the door open.

"Oh. Before I forget, I just have to text Jaz and let her know I won't be home until later." I pull out my phone, wondering if she's started to worry yet or if she's even noticed I'm still not home.

He runs a hand down my side. "You *could* tell her you won't be home at all."

I balk. "You want me to stay the night?"

After wiggling his eyebrows at me playfully, he passes through the living room and leads me into a small kitchen. "I don't hate the idea," he says, standing on his tiptoes to reach a bottle of bourbon on the top shelf of his cabinet.

"You're doing this whole bachelor life thing all wrong, you know?"

He chuckles, twisting the lid off the bottle. It's already been opened, and my skin lines with worry, hot and electric in the air as he pulls down two tumblers from his cabinet. "Do you…have anything else? Still not drinking tonight, if that's okay."

He looks up at me as if he'd forgotten, then snaps his fingers. "That's right. Sorry. I forgot. I've got soda, then. Dr Pepper or root beer, I think. There might be a Pepsi in there, too."

"Root beer sounds delicious." I beam at him, so relieved at how kind he's being when I still worry he thinks that I'm scared he's going to drug me. I mean, I *am* scared of that, but I don't want him to know. *Obvs.*

He winks and pulls a can out of the fridge, passing it to me and pouring his own glass of bourbon and Pepsi. He leans against the counter and takes a sip. Next to him, my eyes land on an orange bottle with green pills inside. I look up, my cheeks flaming hot as I realize I've been caught staring. Somehow, I feel as if I've violated his privacy, though he gives me no hint he's embarrassed. He already told me he's in therapy. If he's taking medicine, too, good for him. The world would be a better place if we were all taking the medicine we need.

"Don't worry," he says, letting the sentence linger. "I was never really interested in being a bachelor, you know? It's not as fun as they make it out to be," he adds, and it takes me a second to realize he's responding to my earlier comment.

I chuckle. "No?"

"Turns out, no." He steps forward, wrapping a hand around my waist, and the air in the room shifts. Tension crackles through the small space between us, and when his eyes flick to my lips, I hold my breath. He lowers his mouth slowly, and just as I start to close my eyes, his lips graze the tip of my nose.

When I open my eyes, he grins. "I've been wanting to do that since we met."

I touch the end of my nose self-consciously. "Kiss my nose?"

He taps it gently. "You have the cutest nose I've ever seen."

I stare at him dubiously. "Is that so?"

He laughs. "I'd never lie to you."

I wrinkle my nose, squinting my eyes playfully, then place my soda down, holding out one hand and pretending to rifle through the pages of an imaginary book with the other.

"What are you doing?" he teases.

"Looking for something..." I search the imaginary page with my finger. "Aha! Just what I thought." I gaze up at him with a twinkle in my eye, a giddy feeling in the pit of my stomach. This man makes me feel like a little kid again, and I've missed that more than I knew. "*The Liar's Handbook*, page three. I knew I'd heard that phrase before."

It takes him a second to catch on to what I've said, but when he does, his jaw drops, and he places his own drink down. "Oh yeah?"

"Right here." I turn my hand around to show him.

He shakes his head, launching forward with a loud laugh. I squeal as he tries to tickle me, chasing me into the living room. We fall on the couch in a fit of laughs, and when I look up, he's too close to me.

Suddenly, nothing feels all that funny anymore.

Instead, there's something different in his eyes. Something warm that I feel under every inch of my skin. Like a current of molten lava coursing through me.

"I'm trying to be a gentleman here," he whispers, his face so close to mine I can feel his breath on my lips. He lifts a hand to brush the hair back from my face, tucking it behind my ear.

I bat my eyelashes at him. "So maybe help a girl out and *stop* doing that."

A growl erupts from the back of his throat and his lips are on mine in an instant, his hand on the side of my head. His kiss is fiery hot and intense. I feel his touch everywhere, his breath everywhere.

I climb over onto his lap, running my fingers through his hair, and he squeezes my hip bones so hard it almost hurts. I roll my hips, grinding against him, and he lets out another groan that I feel directly between my legs.

"Are you sure about this?" His eyes flick over me as if it's his worst fear that I'm going to say no.

In answer, I bite his bottom lip, savoring the taste of him. That seems to be exactly what he was hoping for as he stands, holding me against him with one hand, the other grasping the back of my neck.

He lays me down on the couch and lifts my shirt, trailing kisses over my belly and up my chest.

"I can't believe this is happening," he whispers, his breath tickling my skin.

I look down at him, my body on fire, and grin devilishly. Somehow, I think we both knew this was going to happen. Minutes later, my pants have been peeled off, my shirt is discarded on the floor somewhere, and he's removing the final barrier of his clothes between us.

He trails a finger across my arm as he moves to the end table and opens a drawer, pulling out a condom and a clear bottle of liquid.

"What's that?" I ask, staring at the bottle, heart pounding as I watch him tear open the condom and roll it over himself, his eyes never leaving mine. It's possible he's the most attractive man I've ever been with, and my body seems very aware of that fact. My pulse is thrumming, every atom in my body seeming to call out for him like we're magnetically charged.

"Lube." He turns it around so I can see the label. "Is that okay? I just prefer it."

"Oh, um, sure." I prop myself up on my elbows, hoping the pose looks as sexy as it feels. He pops the top off the bottle and squirts some of the clear liquid into his hand, running it over his length slowly.

My breathing catches as I watch the act in silence. It's the hottest moment of my entire life, and I simultaneously want to watch it forever and hope it ends soon. I need it to end. I need him to kiss me again.

Seeming to sense my eagerness, a smile plays on his lips, and he walks toward me, easing down on the couch over top of my body.

"Hey," he whispers, as every inch of our skin connects.

"Hey," I say with a nervous laugh.

He runs his tongue over his bottom lip before diving back into our kiss. I wrap one leg around him, lifting my pelvis and using my other hand to guide him inside me.

He's cautious at first, gentle, but soon enough, his length fills me wholly. My head goes back as I cry out, the feeling so perfect in this moment I can't believe we had dinner at all.

This is all I actually needed, and I had no idea how badly I did.

I kiss him harder, deeper, and he meets me with the same urgency. My body aches from his harsh touch and the fierceness he's displaying between my legs.

It's almost hurting, but I can't get enough. I've never been with anyone who held me so tightly, like he's afraid I'm going to disappear if he doesn't.

I close my eyes, my head pounding suddenly, and when I open them, it's as if there's no light in the room. My vision is blurry with dark splotches.

I freeze, but he doesn't seem to notice as he continues to thrust into me. His sweaty forehead rests on my chest as he whispers, "That's it, baby. That's it."

I open my mouth to tell him something is wrong, but I can't say anything. No words are coming out of my mouth. No thoughts make sense. "Something's…"

I can't breathe. I feel as if my throat is closing up.

"I…"

I'm going to vomit. I'm going to die. I put a hand on his chest to stop him, but it's as if he doesn't notice. My head spins so fast I don't know which direction is which. I can't make out the shapes in the room, only his blurry face above me.

Something is really, really wrong.

He lifts his head finally, pulling out of me and sitting up. He's staring at me strangely, and then a hint of a smile pulls at one corner of his lips.

"Don't worry," he whispers, grabbing the bottle of lube from above my head and putting more on his fingers before shoving those up inside of me, too. It feels as if I've peed myself from all the warmth and wetness, but I can't move to check. I can't do anything. The slightest movement feels like my head is going to explode. Like it weighs eleven hundred pounds.

I close my eyes again, and they're heavier this time.

I can't go to sleep.

I have to fight.

If I go to sleep, I'll die.

But as I feel his fingers working me, hear the squirt of the bottle as he applies more and more of whatever is inside of it, my head starts to slip. Like the first moments of turbulence in flight, I feel my stomach catch, and I hold my breath.

I don't know if I'm physically falling or if it's all in my head.

I squeeze my eyes shut and brace for impact, and then…I'm gone.

CHAPTER TWENTY-SEVEN

5—1:22:27

The memory comes back to me like an unexpected ocean wave, stealing the breath from my lungs and knocking me off my feet. I'm vaguely aware of Elliot standing above me, begging me for answers I don't have.

"I remember what happened," I tell him, barely managing to choke the words out. "I remember how I got here."

"You do?" His eyes widen as he stares at me. "You know who he is?"

I nod, the memories replaying in my mind, bitter and scorching. "I did everything right," I whisper, touching my neck. "This wasn't my fault." The relief, the apology to myself after days of feeling so angry with my actions, is a balm to my wounds. "I did *everything* right. Everything they tell you to do. I told someone where I was. I didn't drink anything that could've been contaminated, but…" I blink back tears, looking up at him. "In the end, it didn't matter. In the end, he tricked me. He *planned* for me. He counted on me outsmarting him. And I let him. I fell for it."

"This is not your fault," Elliot says feverishly, touching my shoulders. "Whatever happened, it is not your fault."

"But it is. I told him your name. We were on a date, and I mentioned your name when he asked about previous heartbreaks. I'm the only reason you're here." I cover my face with my hands. "This is all my fault."

"It is not your fault," he says again. "No matter what happens, you didn't bring me here." He pulls me into his chest, wrapping his arms around me. "It's not your fault, Soph. Do you hear me?"

I open my mouth to respond, but before I can, there's a clicking sound in the distance and the door flings open. We both jump back as the guard from earlier stalks into the room, staring at the two of us as if we're the most shocking thing he's ever seen.

"What the hell are you doing here?" he demands, waving his hands out to the sides. "What did you do?"

"Nothing," I tell him, thinking quickly. "Someone came to our house and attacked us. He got hurt, and we ran here looking for help."

He crosses his arms. "I have to take you back."

"We're not going anywhere. Didn't you hear her? Some lunatic tried to attack us, and we had to fight back. He's at the house where you've been keeping us.

He's hurt, and someone needs to go there and help him, but it won't be us. Take us somewhere else. Anywhere else."

The man shakes his head, pulling out a pair of cuffs. "Let's go. I have strict orders. You're not allowed to be out here alone."

"You're not listening!" Elliot shouts. "A man is hurt!"

"The man has been taken care of," the guard cuts him off. "Hand me the key you took."

"We don't have a key," Elliot says.

"Stop lying. Hand me the key now." The man's voice is cutting. He grabs my arm, tugging me against him. "Or she'll be punished."

Elliot meets my eyes, swallowing, and slowly reaches into his pocket. With a grim expression, he drops the key into the man's outstretched palm.

The man tucks it into his pocket and spins me around to face him. "Now hand me your wrists, or I will take them by force."

My knife is still on the desk next to the computer, but there's no chance I can reach it in time. My throat constricts, and I hold out my hands. His attention is pointed toward me as he hooks the cuff to my wrist and leads me out the door, always keeping an eye on Elliot, who is close behind us. Elliot could try to stab him, but we both know it wouldn't work. That possibility disappears anyway when the man notices Elliot's knife and confiscates it, draining my last ounce of hope. Like before, we're strapped to a golf cart and forced to sit and wait while the guard returns inside to hang a towel over the window and radio to someone about what's happened.

"Did he leave a key?" Elliot asks, keeping his voice low.

I don't even have to look, because I already did. It was my first thought, too. "No. He took it with him."

He curses under his breath. "We were so close to getting out of here. We never should've stuck around. I should've made us leave immediately after you sent that email. We knew it was only a matter of time until they figured out we were missing."

I know, but I also know it's probably my fault that we did. I was so desperate to hear from Jaz that I didn't think about anything else. I felt safe in that space, protected for just a moment.

When the guard returns, the golf cart sinks with his weight, and he starts it up, backing out without a word. As we near the woods, I hear a voice, and it takes me several seconds to realize it's him.

"Listen to me. There are cameras everywhere here," he says. "They can see you everywhere you go, including the offices."

My eyes squint to see him better in the dim, night light. "Okay?" At this point, I kind of already assumed as much.

"Stop being stupid," he says. "Stop sneaking out. Stop fighting this. It'll only make it worse in the end."

"Make what worse?"

"You're...entertaining, Sophie," he says, and there's a hint of something I didn't expect in his voice. Warmth, maybe. Or appreciation.

"What the fuck is that supposed to mean?" Elliot asks, not bothering to hide the tinge of jealousy in his tone.

"It's not a good thing," the man says in a sharp whisper, then he lowers his voice even more. "Look, they control everything. They watch everything. What you've been doing to escape will never work."

I feel something brush my thigh and look down to spot his hand next to me. He pulls his fingers back slowly, and I catch the hint of metal on the vinyl seat.

A key.

He has given me the key back.

I pick it up. "What is this for—"

"Hide it," he says. "Hide it, and don't take it out until fifty-nine exactly."

"Fifty-nine?" I tuck the key into my pocket. "What are you talking about?"

"Think about it," he says. "And stop talking."

"Why should we trust you?" I touch the ends of my chopped hair. "After what you did."

He nods slowly, his eyes cutting to look at me for just a second as if that's all he'll allow himself. "Trust me, if it was anyone else who'd been there, your punishment would've been a lot worse. Now stop talking, or I won't be able to protect you."

CHAPTER TWENTY-EIGHT

5—1:22:15

I can't believe it, but the guard was right about Nick. By the time we're forcibly delivered back to the little blue house, all signs that he was ever here have been removed. There's not a drop of blood or sign of a struggle in sight, though the whole place reeks of bleach and cleaner.

I cover my nose with my shirt as the scent stings my eyes.

The guard ushers us in the door with a pointed nod and leaves, locking it behind him. Though I desperately want to, Elliot and I can't talk about anything that has happened or anything the guard told us. We can't discuss whether or not we should trust him. We know *they're* watching—whoever they are—and we know they're listening.

I eye the countdown clock on the wall. It's the only thing that makes sense for the 'fifty-nine' message to have been about.

We still have fifteen minutes if I'm right, so I head into the bathroom to freshen up and splash water on my face. I leave the door open in case Elliot wants to talk, and he follows me in after a second's hesitation.

"You good?" he asks, his words as strained as my thoughts feel. Knowing we're being watched puts extra pressure on everything. I feel as if we're contestants on a show we aren't being paid for and never agreed to star in. This is why I hate reality TV.

I dry my face on a hand towel before turning to look his way. "No." There's no point in denying it. "But I will be."

He has his shirt back on now and the drying blood on its fabric is a painful reminder of how much we've gone through. His hand is bloody as he stretches it out to brush my pinkie and the small gesture is sweet and meaningful in a way I hadn't expected.

"Are you?"

"I've been better," he jokes dryly.

Back in the kitchen, we fill glasses of water and gulp them down. I hadn't realized how thirsty I was. My eyes trail the room and land on the bag of popcorn on the couch. As much as I want to eat something, the nerves in my stomach won't let me.

Something is going to happen in less than fifteen minutes, but I don't know what. Is that when they'll come for us? Is that when we'll die? Was him giving me the key some sort of trap? Or trick? Like telling Nick to kill his dad in order to escape and then upping the payment and asking him to kill us, too?

Whatever it is, I don't believe this is anything fake or set up. The knife Nick had was very real. He could've seriously harmed us, and obviously, Elliot *really* did harm him. Despite it all, I hope he's okay. I hope they were able to get to him in time.

I'm not sure I want to know, though, either way. It's too scary.

Whatever is going on, the stakes couldn't be more real.

I walk across the room and watch the clock count down. When it lands on 22:00, I hold my breath and count silently to myself.

1
2
3
4
5
6
7
8
9
10
11
12
13
14
15

16
17
18
19
20
21
22
23
24
25
26
27
28
29
30
31
32
33
34
35
36
37
38
39
40
41
42
43
44

45

46

47

48

49

50

51

52

59

My timing was off. It's time. It's here—*21:59.*

For half a second, I wait. For what, I'm not sure. An explosion, maybe. For the walls of our set to collapse. For my friends and family to run in and tell us this has all been a joke. For the man to come in and finally kill us.

When none of that happens, I suck in a deep breath, pull the key out of my pocket and make my way toward the door slowly, eyes peeled for anything and everything to go wrong.

When I swing open the door, there's a golf cart pulling up in the distance. My heart stops in my chest, threatening death, before I realize it's the same guard again.

The one I so desperately want to trust but am still not sure I can, especially after what he did to me. I touch my hair again. Was he being honest when he said someone else would've done worse? I shiver at the thought.

"Come on. Come on." He waves furiously for us to hurry and join him on the cart.

"What is happening?" I whisper-shout, rushing toward him and jumping onto the golf cart with Elliot close behind.

"There's a three-minute window every time the clock gets to fifty-nine minutes where all the house cameras go down. Where no one is watching you. That's all the time we have to get you to the fence. It's not enough, but it'll have to do. I'll get you as close as I can."

"If you were coming back, why give us the key?"

"I didn't know if I'd make it back. I was going to try, but I wanted to give you a chance to escape before your countdown went off either way." He slams on the gas, and we take off, the wind whipping through our hair—or, rather, what's left of it. "I couldn't tell you about the time and risk anyone hearing me."

"Why are you helping us?" Elliot asks.

"I don't know," the guard says with a growl. "Trust me, I wish I did."

"Can you tell us what is going on here?"

He shakes his head. "Get down and stay still until I tell you to move. The cameras out here still work fine. They won't be watching them, but if they realize something is up, they can. If they do that..." He trails off, chewing his bottom lip. "We'll all be in trouble."

"Can you at least tell us your name?"

"Adam," he says with a breath. "I'm Adam. Now get down."

We do as we're told, hunkering down in the golf cart.

Eventually, we stop, and I realize we're at the office again.

"What are we doin—"

"Shh!" He cuts me off with a hand to the mouth and nods his head. In the distance, there are flashlights. A boulder settles in my gut. "Go!" he whispers, pointing toward the office. "Hurry."

We scurry off of the golf cart and sprint up the stairs. Quickly, he unlocks the door and shoves it open. "Find somewhere to hide. Now."

Elliot and I scramble through the doorway, searching for any place to hide. My chest goes tight when I notice the knife I left on the desk is missing now. I open the door to a small metal armoire and step inside of it. The door groans as I close it, and I squeeze my eyes shut with a wince. The small space smells of iron and body odor, and I peer through the cracks, watching as Elliot slides under the desk and back into a corner of the room. I wished desperately that we'd been able to hide together, but in the moment, we both had just one thing on our minds: *get to safety imme-diately.*

Footsteps on the porch send my pulse racing, and a few moments later, I hear the door open.

"What are you, a vampire? Why are you hanging out

in the dark, you creep?" a man's voice says with a laugh. It's a voice I don't recognize.

"I was checking the cameras," Adam says.

"Did you see them?" That voice belongs to the main masked man, the leader. Our captor. I'd know it anywhere by now.

"Nothing yet." He clicks his tongue. Adam is a much better actor than Robert was, and I couldn't be more thankful for it.

"We'll find 'em," the leader says. "Ain't no way outta here. They're around here somewhere." The wickedness in his voice is palpable in the room. It's thick and evil, the kind of evil some people are lucky enough to never know. "And when we do…" He begins to pace the room, whistling that familiar tune.

CHAPTER TWENTY-NINE

"When they do, we'll squash 'em like pigs," one of the other guards says, oinking loudly to prove the point.

"Ah, no. Nothing like that," the leader says. "I'd rather offer them a deal. If they're anywhere around here, I'd like to get a message to them." The inflection in his tone tells me we've been caught. This is over. He may not know where we are in the room, but he knows we're here. It will take mere seconds for them to find us in this small space. "If one of them comes out and tells us where the other is hiding, that person can leave and go home. No questions asked."

Adam shakes his head, standing from the chair in front of the computer desk. "I've told you. They're not here."

The leader—Big D, I'm assuming—with his familiar voice, clicks his tongue. Ghosts of his fingers dance over my skin in my memory, and I clasp my throat.

"Here, piggy, piggy, piggy," he calls, his voice low, slow, and menacing. I feel every syllable in my nerves, like he's whispering directly against my skin. "Come out, come out, little piggy."

My eyes dart across the room to where Elliot is hiding, and I wish we were together more than ever now. I wish he could hold my hand and tell me everything is going to be okay, that whatever comes, at least we're in this together.

At this moment, more than anything, I'm just so grateful I've had him with me through this. I'm so grateful for the small kindness of having a friend with me in the end.

Adam walks in front of the armoire, bathing me in his shadow for just a moment, and as he passes, I watch as the man removes his mask, pulling it up over his head slowly.

It's him. If there was any doubt left, it's completely gone now. In front of me stands the charming man who made me laugh just days ago on our date. The man I trusted enough to let into my body.

"Sophie? Sophie, honey? Can you hear me? I told you, I'm a gentleman, remember? I haven't hurt you, have I? I haven't harmed you in any way since you arrived, and I won't. I've had so much fun with you, and you're special. That's why you're here, because I see that." He pauses, spinning in circles, his eyes landing on every space of the room. When they land on the armoire where I'm hiding, my heart skips a beat.

"Now, look, I don't want to hurt you, but I meant what I said to you in that message in the bathroom, and I mean what I'm saying now. Only one of you gets to go home. One person from each house. I want it to be you, but that means you have to come out and tell us where Elliot is. Tell us where he is, do nothing else, and you can go home. It's that simple. I know you must miss Jaz. And she must be missing you, too. Just come out, tell us where to find Elliot, the man who broke your heart, and this is all over. He doesn't deserve you, Sophie. You know that. He's shown you who he is."

I cover my mouth to stifle my sob as he picks at my deepest, most raw wound. Next to him, Adam shifts uncomfortably.

"What's wrong with you? Have you grown to care for her?" the man sneers.

Adam swallows, squaring his shoulders and looking like a soldier in stature. "Of course not."

"Then tell the boy to come out. Tell Elliot. Tell one of them so this can all be over."

Adam shakes his head again, still not meeting his eyes. "I have no idea where they are, Darrell. I told you."

Something shifts across the room, and I see everyone turning before I realize what's happening. Before I see Elliot come into view. When I do, my heart drops.

In front of me, Elliot is standing, moving. He's not looking at where I'm hiding, but directly at Darrell.

He's going to give himself up to save me.

He comes fully out of his hiding spot, and Darrell beams at him. "Well, well, well. You're not who I expected to see, I've got to be honest."

Elliot squares his shoulders, takes a deep breath, and points across the room to where I'm hiding in the armoire. "You want us to play the game? Fine. She's in there. Now let me go home."

CHAPTER THIRTY

She's in there. Now let me go home.

His words echo in my ears. Another broken promise. Another betrayal. He said we'd get through this together. He lied.

Instantly, the lights come on, turning the windows into mirrors with the room reflected in their glass. Darrell's eyes widen with delight, and he rubs his hands together as if he's about to devour a delicious meal as he walks toward the armoire.

I hold my breath, trying to think as he flings open the door I'm hiding behind. My safe space has been invaded. He smiles at me, his eyes crinkling in the corners. The familiarity of it stings the most.

"Hey," he whispers, that word in his voice reminiscent of that night on his couch.

I fill my mouth with spit and hawk it at him, so filled with fury, it's brimming over. He grins, wiping the spit away from his eye slowly, completely unbothered. He holds out his hand, palm upturned. "Come with me."

Across the room, Elliot won't look at me. His jaw is set as hard as stone as he studies the floor like it's a painted masterpiece in a museum. No one has ever looked at a floor harder than he is currently looking at this floor.

Darrell grins at Adam next. "Nice work." He high-fives him. "You get better every time. They really believed you were helping them." Darrell spins around, holding his hands out to his sides, and the other guards begin to clap. "Give the man an Oscar," he declares, patting him on the back with obvious pride.

It was all an act. Everything. Every moment with Adam as he tried to garner our trust. It was all an act that would lead us here, to this moment. If Elliot and I wouldn't kill each other directly, they'd find another way to make it happen.

Darrell nods at Adam. "Go back and contact the winner."

Without a word or a single, solitary glance in my direction, Adam walks out of the room, followed by one of the other guards, leaving Elliot and me alone with Darrell and two guards. These two are still wearing masks.

"Winner?" Elliot asks, brows furrowed as he looks at Darrell.

Darrell clasps his hands together in front of him,

turning to pace the room. "Yes." He taps his lips with one finger. "I guess I should explain some things to you, hmm? Let's see, where do we start? Well, by now, you know you've been recorded from the moment you arrived at my farm. You can thank Sophie for your arrival. She's the one who gave me your name—still a bit hung up on your break-up." He gives an exaggerated frown. "From the moment she said your name, we were working on digging up every bit of dirt we could find on the both of you. Text message history, social media, medical records, the works. As you've now seen, we're incredibly thorough in our search, and lucky us, there's always dirt to be found. But I'm rambling. Thanks to our games, you already know all of that." He waves his hand. "But what you don't know is that you've been the star of your own little reality show, only it's one where the stakes are much higher."

"What are you talking about?" I growl. My stomach clenches as if I'm going to be sick. That's how they knew about my time in the hospital and about Elliot and Caroline.

I can't draw in a deep enough breath.

Either oblivious to or completely ignoring my panic, Darrell goes on, "Everything that has happened to you, everything that you've experienced since you arrived, has been live streamed for hundreds of viewers online. They've been able to buy experiences for you, like your snacks and puzzles. They've been able to bet on things like when you would finally give in and eat, where you'd sleep, what you'd drink, if you would try to attack me, if you two would sleep together"—he wiggles a finger between us—"if Robert or Nick would betray you first, if you'd actually try to climb the fence, if you'd trust Adam, and so on. You get the picture. Every action you've taken, everything you've done or not done since you arrived, has been the work of our viewers—our bidders—and slowly, they've been able to work their way down to just one winner. And now, that winner gets to decide your fate."

"What the fuck are you talking about?" Elliot asks. "How is any of this legal? Who was the winner? And when do I get to leave?"

"Oh, it's certainly not legal. And, as far as you leaving, well, I'm afraid I may have fibbed a little bit about that." Darrell smiles again bitterly. "You see, the final contest was a bet on who would rat out the other person. Neither of you were going to leave, but one of you would win a fate decided by someone else, and one of you would win a fate decided by me." He looks at the man standing next to him and tilts his head toward Elliot.

In a second, the man pulls a knife and slits Elliot's throat.

As simple as if he'd been checking the time.

A line forms across the pale skin on his Adam's apple, growing dark with blood as it begins to pour out of the wound and drip down his neck and onto the collar of his shirt. His eyes find mine, and he opens his mouth to speak, but no words come out.

I can't move. I'm frozen as I watch him fall to his knees. I let out a bloodcurdling scream, covering my mouth as my worst nightmare unfolds right in front of me.

No one else in the room flinches.

Elliot is dying.

I have to do something.

He's dying right in front of me, and I'm the only one who can save him.

Except, I can't. I'm powerless. Helpless to do anything.

In front of me, Darrell seems to take pleasure in knowing that. His evil face wrinkles with a disgusting smile. I can't believe I ever thought he was handsome. How could I look at him and see anything but the emptiness I see now?

I'm hyperventilating, staring at Elliot's crumpled body, when Darrell asks, "Do you know much about the dark web, Sophie?"

I stare at him with tears in my eyes. This is impossible. This, more than anything else, has to be a dream. A nightmare that I can't wake up from.

Wake up.

Wake up.

Wake up.

Jesus Christ, Sophie, please wake up.

The men bend over and pick up Elliot's body. His

mouth is still gasping for air like a fish out of water as they drag him from the room.

I can't think. Can't breathe. Can't see. None of this is real. It can't be real.

"How could you do this?" I demand. "How can you kill him?"

"It's the way the game works, unfortunately." He gives me a look of regret.

"A game *you* orchestrate."

He nods. "It was either him or you, Sophie. Only one of you was leaving, no matter what. Frankly, you should be relieved with how things turned out."

"Relieved that my life is now in the hands of some stranger? Who won, anyway?" I ask, wrapping my arms around myself. "What is he going to do to me?"

"I'm afraid this is where my involvement ends. Once your winner arrives, they can decide what they want to do with you. You will belong to them. Take Adam, for example. Someone chose for his fate to be that he works for me for the rest of his life. I sort of hope you'll get a similar fate. You'll find I have plenty of ways to entertain." His eyes rake over my body, and I feel the path as real as an ice cube on my skin. How could I have ever looked at him and not seen the monster within?

There's a knock at the door, and Darrell's eyes light up. "Oh, that means we have news. Wait here." He goes to the door and returns a moment later. "Your winner has chosen to meet you at a hotel. We've let him know you'll want to"—his eyes travel over me again, this time with disgust—*"freshen up* first." He holds a hand out. "One of the guards will take you to him. Then you're free to go. Have a nice life, Sophie. You really brought so much entertainment to my viewers, and I can't thank you enough."

I press my lips together and walk past him. A guard leads me to a car waiting outside, and I climb in, all fight lost as I process everything that has happened.

"Wake up! We're here."

The harsh voice jerks me from sleep, and I sit up, looking around. For just a moment, I was somewhere far away from here. Somewhere peaceful and safe.

Of course, that couldn't last long enough. I look out the window of the car, the lights of the hotel's sign blinding me. The building is nicer than I expected, though I suppose whoever this man is, he must have money to have been able to bid so much for me.

I try to imagine this could be some sort of billionaire romance story like I've read before, that he saw me and fell in love, and somehow this is all going to work out. Though I know it's impossible, I hold on to the fantasy as we enter the hotel.

Every minute of happiness that I can hold on to, I will because I assume my future doesn't have much happiness left.

The hotel is several stories high and one I don't recognize. As we enter the building, I realize I have no idea what city we're in.

Once we're inside, the guard leads me to the elevator and up to the sixth floor. We find room 613 and he knocks three times before stepping away. When he leaves my side, I consider bolting with what energy I have left, but there isn't time.

The door swings open, and I pray this man, whoever he is, will show me mercy. Except when I see the face waiting for me, my heart squeezes, and I'm nearly sure I'm still asleep and dreaming.

It has to be a dream.

My best friend beams at me, her dark, spiral curls gathered around her head, her perfect brown skin like a figment of my imagination. When something bad happens to you, sometimes your mind reverts to something happier to protect you. I've heard about it, but never experienced it until now. That must be what this is, but if it is, I'm okay with it. I'd rather spend my last moments with her, even if it's only inside the confines of my mind.

Jaz grabs my arm and pulls me into the room without a word, and when the door shuts, she wraps me into her arms and squeezes me like it's the last time she'll ever see me. Her coconut and vanilla scent fills my nostrils, and I inhale deeply, wanting so desperately for it to be real.

"Sophie..." she whispers, and it's enough to make

me think this might not be a figment of my imagination. She feels so real against my skin.

I'm stunned into silence, and when she pulls back, rubbing her hands down along my face, it seems she is too. Her chestnut eyes fill with tears as she stares at me.

"I can't believe it's you."

"*I* can't believe it's *you*," I say back. "Are you real?" If this is all a dream, I'm okay with it. I'm okay with this being my last memory, and I wish I'd kept those pills from the box. I would take them right now and die happy in her arms.

"I'm real." She runs her hands over my skin to prove the point. "I'm so real. You scared me to death. I was so scared I'd never see you again." She smiles through her tears.

I blink. "I…I don't understand. How is this happening? How are you here?"

She's hugging me again, choking back fresh tears as she says, "I will tell you everything, but is there anything you need first? Do you want to go to the hospital? Did they hurt you? Are you starving? Tell me what you need, and I will get it for you."

"I need to know what happened," I blurt out, more anger in my tone than I meant for there to be.

"I…I won you," she says softly, chewing her bottom lip as she winces. "When you left…Sophie, I went crazy when I couldn't find you. I threatened so many security guards to get footage of who you were with that night. I contacted the police, who were absolutely no help to positively no one's surprise. They said you were probably just off on a date, but I knew better. I knew you would call. You'd call…" She wipes her tears away, then runs her hands through what's left of my hair. Someday, I'll have to explain that to her, but I'm not ready yet. I don't think I could summon my voice if my life depended on it. "I was on my own, and I didn't know what to do. I ended up logging into your cloud, and I found your messages with DJ. It took so much digging, like, I'm probably on a watchlist somewhere. And I've pissed off the entire police department, so please don't ever get a ticket, but I finally found out who he was. Darrell Johnson. I went to the apartment where he'd been staying and convinced his super that I was his lawyer, and he was in jail, and I needed to get something for him. I broke so many laws." She's crying harder and so am I, and suddenly we're on the floor, and I don't know how we got here.

"But I found him, which led me to some dark places online. And then…I found you. I saw you on the screen of this fucked-up game where we could bid on you. Like, stupid shit. I paid six hundred bucks to send you a box of things you loved, but I threw in some weird things you didn't like so no one got suspicious I actually knew you. We had to bet on things you'd do. Would you eat the snacks? Would you eat the food they brought? Or use the toothpaste that they drugged to get you both to pass out. Would you take a shower? Would you sleep with Elliot? Would you kill Elliot?

What would you do if Elliot disappeared for a day? It was all weird and so messed up, but at the end of the day, I *knew* you. I moved through the game quickly. I just wanted to bring you home, no matter what it cost, but I might be late on rent for a while." She snorts, and I can't be mad at her, because it's so Jaz to make a joke at a time like this. "Soph, I was so scared to tell the police once I found out what was going on. I probably should have, but I worried they'd send up some alert, and the entire thing would go away, and I'd lose you forever. The only way I knew to get you back was to play the game, and so I did. There were only three of us left when we bet on whether you'd turn in Elliot or he'd turn you in, but I knew you wouldn't."

She hugs me, kissing my cheek. I can't believe it. "I love you," I blurt out. The only words I can muster. The weight of everything that has happened, of everything she's told me, of my complicated feelings for Elliot returning, of learning how he slept with Caroline, of his final betrayal. The weight of his death, of his blood spilling out on the floor in front of me. The pain and the loss and the exhaustion and the raw, intense grief and processing of everything that has happened over the past few days hits me all at once. I was raped. I was kidnapped. I was violated in every way. People watched me. They made a game out of my horror, my pain.

My hair. I lift a hand to touch it. It's the last thing that matters right now, but it's the thing that breaks me. The final straw on this camel's back.

I crumple in her arms, and she understands. She's there for me like I always hoped she would be. If this is real, this is everything.

My body is hollow as I collapse against her, letting the wail escape my lungs for the first time, the scream I've been holding in for days. She doesn't silence me or ask me to be quiet or to explain. She's seen it all. She knows exactly what I've gone through.

She knows.

She holds me and rubs my back and rocks me right there on the floor, whispering in my ear. "I love you. I love you. I love you."

It's the lullaby I drift in and out to, my consciousness coming in waves, like flickers of a flame. I have no idea how long we remain on that floor as images flash in my mind. Elliot's blood. Nick's blood. The sting of Elliot walking out of his hiding place, of him pointing in my direction.

The look on Nick's face when he came at me with the knife.

The burn of the branches as I ran through the woods. The pain of returning to the house, of being caught, of being trapped time after time.

"I can't believe you did that. I can't believe any of this," I whisper, hugging her tightly. What I mean is: *Why would you do any of this? How hard must you have worked to find me? Was it worth it? Am I worth it?*

I should've fought harder. I should've saved myself.

I should've never trusted Elliot. But also—I never wanted him to die. I never wanted anyone to die.

"When I got your email," she says with a deep, soul-crushing frown, "it killed me. It killed me knowing you thought I could ever give up on you." She holds my cheeks, staring at me with tears pouring down her face. "I could never, would never, give up on you. You are my best friend, the love of my life, and the person I refuse to live without. Do you hear me? I will take down the entire dark web if that's what it takes to bring you home to me."

She brings her lips to mine then, and we cry and hug, and I wail some more, sobbing through the relief, through the pain, through the fury, unable to decide what to do or feel first. Nothing is okay, and I have so many questions left and so much to work through, but for the moment, none of it matters. For the first time in so long, here with my best friend, with the person who single-handedly fought for me and dragged me back home with her bare hands, I know I'm safe. I know I'm home.

And for the first time in several days, there's no place else I'd rather be. I slide my hand down my side, pinching myself just to be certain, but I know I'm awake, and I know this is real.

No dream has ever been this perfect.

CHAPTER THIRTY-ONE

THREE YEARS LATER

It's not enough. I've put my heart and soul into this company, into finding online predators and protecting men and women across the world, but it's not enough.

I stare down into the face of yet another missing girl who went on a date and never came home. It's not Darrell—Jaz and I fought tooth and nail to make sure he was caught. He's awaiting sentencing, but for now, this time at least, it's not him.

Still, it's someone else. Someone worse, maybe.

Jaz walks up behind me, rubbing her hand across my back. "Are you ready?"

She can sense that I'm upset without me saying a word. She knows me. She really, truly knows me. To be known by another person in this way, in a way that doesn't feel like a risk, but something as stable and simple as the ground underneath my feet, is the safest a person can feel in a world full of danger.

More than that, she chose me, and that's all I've ever really wanted. To be chosen by someone who unequivocally has my back.

I nod finally, giving her the reassurance I can. "I'll be okay."

"I know you will." She runs her thumb over my cheek. "You're a fighter."

The line is cheesy, considering that's exactly what our company is called. A company that has saved thousands of girls and stopped online predators in their tracks from the date of its inception. But somehow, it works every time she says it.

Every single time those words leave her mouth, I feel ten feet tall, like I can take on anything. And in this line of work, that's a necessity.

We can't save the world ourselves, I know, but that doesn't mean we won't try. It doesn't mean I'll ever give up on those girls and guys who've been taken advantage of by someone online because I know what it feels like to have someone at home rooting for you. I never want anyone to go through the experience I did, or anything like it, and have to question whether or not someone is looking for them.

The room we're in grows silent as the lights dim and an announcer comes up onto the stage to introduce me. I've done this a thousand times, but I never get less nervous. Every single time, I think about quitting.

But I can't. People are counting on me, and I've

never felt the pure determination that brings me before we created this company.

Jaz squeezes my hand and kisses my cheek. "You've got this."

I grin at her, squaring my shoulders and sucking in a long, deep inhale. When the crowd begins to clap and the spotlight pans toward where I'm set to make my entrance, I lift my hand in the air, stepping out onto the stage like a politician, a smile plastered on my face.

I reach the lectern and adjust the microphone, allowing the applause to quiet down before I look up at the crowd. "Thank you so much for that warm welcome. I'm Sophie Thatcher, owner and founder of Fighter, and I'm here to tell you my story. I have to warn you, it gets a little dark, but don't worry"—I grin at Jaz where she stands off stage, one hand on her chest, beaming with pride—"we're going to get through it together."

WOULD YOU RECOMMEND THE HIDDEN?

If you enjoyed this story, please consider leaving me a quick review. It doesn't have to be long—just a few words will do. Who knows? Your review might be the thing that encourages a future reader to take a chance on my work!

To leave a review, please find your favorite retailer at the link on my website:
kierstenmodglinauthor.com/thehidden

Let everyone know how much you loved
The Hidden on Goodreads:
https://bit.ly/kmodglinthehidden

STAY UP TO DATE ON EVERYTHING KMOD!

Thank you so much for reading this story. I'd love to invite you to sign up for my mailing list and text alerts so we can be sure you don't miss my next release.
Sign up for my mailing list here:
kierstenmodglinauthor.com/nlsignup

Sign up for my text alerts here:
kierstenmodglinauthor.com/textalerts

ACKNOWLEDGMENTS

For me, *The Hidden* is a story about trust. Trusting ourselves, trusting others, and deciding to trust again even when we've been burned. Trust is never something that has come easily for me and, for that reason, this was an especially interesting and delicate topic to play with in this story.

This is one of my few books where the initial idea came to me in a dream, of all places. I had a very vivid dream about being trapped in a house just like the one in the story, about escaping and discovering the rest of the dark secrets that lurked in the woods, but unlike Sophie's story, my dream ended shortly after meeting "the others" (trying to keep spoilers to a minimum here!). When I woke up the next morning, I immediately jotted this idea down for future use, but I had no idea where I would take it—or, more honestly, where it would take me.

With this story, I wanted Sophie (and you) to doubt everyone around her. I wanted her to doubt herself. I wanted to explore the ways we come back from our worst moments, the people that come into or lives in the most unexpected circumstances, and how we decide whom to trust and when to forgive. Most of all, I wanted to play with the ideas of intuition and how we learn to trust ourselves again.

This story was such a wild journey for me, right along with Sophie. From the beginning, I identified with her in so many ways and rooted for her to find her way to freedom, all while discovering the truth about what was happening and who she was.

Sometimes, in the darkest times, we have to be our own source of light. And sometimes, it's okay to lean on the ones who have earned our trust (even when that's really, really hard!)

Thank you so much for going on this adventure with me. As always, this story wouldn't have made it to your hands without the support, advice, belief, and encouragement of the following people:

To my husband and daughter—thank you both so much for being the best part of my days. Thank you for loving me, for celebrating with me, for cheering me on, for letting me disappear for hours in the writing cave at the most inopportune times, and for being here every step of the way. You guys have seen it all—the good, the bad, the really beautiful, and the terribly scary—and I couldn't do it without you. I love you both beyond measure.

To my editor, Sarah West—thank you for seeing and believing in my stories through all the rubble and mess. Thank you for your insights, advice, ridiculous knowledge of the English language, and wisdom. I'm forever grateful to have had you on my team from the very beginning. What a journey this has been!

To the proofreading team at My Brother's Editor—thank you for being my final set of eyes and polishing each story until it shines!

To my loyal readers (AKA the #KMod Squad)—I don't even know where to start. Thank you for everything. Thank you for returning story after story with no loss of enthusiasm. Thank you for cheering me on, for the emails, the social media tags, the recommendations to your friends and family, the camaraderie you've created within our Squad, the pure joy you have for my characters, and the way you've given my wild ideas a safe space to land. For a little girl who never felt truly understood, you guys have made me feel more seen, loved, and appreciated than I ever believed possible. I dreamed of you, I wished for you, and still, I could've never imagined how amazing you'd be. Thank you for being here and for making all of this possible. I will be forever grateful for all you've given me.

To my book club/gang/besties—Sara, both Erins, Heather, Dee, and June—the best people I know. Thank you for being the source of so much laughter, safety, and love. Thank you for the inside jokes that will always be funny. Thank you for being here for me for the ups, downs, and everything in between. Thank you for being a safe space of strong, smart women, where everything is free of judgment and we can not only be ourselves but be celebrated for that. I've never experienced such true friendship and I can't thank you ladies enough for coming into my life and changing everything. Love you bunches! CHEERIO!

To my bestie, Emerald O'Brien—thank you for so so much more than I could ever put into words. What a journey we've been on together! From the young women in 2018 and 2019, shamelessly sharing our hopes and dreams with each other in the quiet moments when we felt so unseen by the rest of the world, to the women now who would be so proud to see what we've been able to make happen. We opened our own doors, built our own tables, and those younger women wouldn't believe the houses we've crafted brick by brick, story by story. I love you, I'm grateful for you. No one in this world knows me like you do and no one accepts me like you do. I'm so grateful for your friendship, your wisdom, and the light you bring to this world. Same moon, my friend. Always.

To my audiobook publishing team at Dreamscape—thank you for helping to get my stories into the hands of as many readers as possible!

Last but certainly not least, to you, dear reader—thank you for being here! Thank you for purchasing this story and supporting my art and my dreams. In a world full of distractions where I know you could've spent this time doing anything else, it means the world that we were able to go on this adventure together. I sincerely hope you enjoyed this story as much as I loved writing it for you. Without you, none of this is possible. As always, whether this was your first Kiersten Modglin book or your 47th, I hope this journey was everything you hoped for and nothing like you expected.

ABOUT THE AUTHOR

KIERSTEN MODGLIN is a #1 bestselling author of psychological thrillers. Her books have sold over 1.5 million copies and been translated into multiple languages. Kiersten is a member of International Thriller Writers, Novelists, Inc., and the Alliance of Independent Authors. She is a KDP Select All-Star and a recipient of *ThrillerFix*'s Best Psychological Thriller Award, *Suspense Magazine*'s Best Book of 2021 Award, a 2022 Silver Falchion for Best Suspense, and a 2022 Silver Falchion for Best Overall Book of 2021. Kiersten grew up in rural western Kentucky and later relocated to Nashville, Tennessee, where she now lives with her family. Kiersten's readers across the world lovingly refer to her as "KMod." A binge-watching expert, psychology fanatic, and *indoor* enthusiast, Kiersten enjoys rainy days spent with her favorite people and evenings with her nose in a book.

Sign up for Kiersten's newsletter here:
kierstenmodglinauthor.com/nlsignup

Sign up for text alerts from Kiersten here:
kierstenmodglinauthor.com/textalerts

kierstenmodglinauthor.com
www.facebook.com/kierstenmodglinauthor
www.facebook.com/groups/kmodsquad
www.threads.net/kierstenmodglinauthor
www.instagram.com/kierstenmodglinauthor
www.tiktok.com/@kierstenmodglinauthor
www.goodreads.com/kierstenmodglinauthor
www.bookbub.com/authors/kiersten-modglin

ALSO BY KIERSTEN MODGLIN

STANDALONE NOVELS

Becoming Mrs. Abbott

The List

The Missing Piece

Playing Jenna

The Beginning After

The Better Choice

The Good Neighbors

The Lucky Ones

I Said Yes

The Mother-in-Law

The Dream Job

The Nanny's Secret

The Liar's Wife

My Husband's Secret

The Perfect Getaway

The Roommate

The Missing

Just Married

Our Little Secret

Widow Falls

Missing Daughter

The Reunion

Tell Me the Truth

The Dinner Guests

If You're Reading This…

A Quiet Retreat

The Family Secret

Don't Go Down There

Wait for Dark

You Can Trust Me

Hemlock

Do Not Open

You'll Never Know I'm Here

The Stranger

The Hollow

Bitter House

The Guilty One

The Hidden

ARRANGEMENT TRILOGY

The Arrangement (Book 1)

The Amendment (Book 2)

The Atonement (Book 3)

THE MESSES SERIES

The Cleaner (Book 1)

The Healer (Book 2)

The Liar (Book 3)

The Prisoner (Book 4)

NOVELLAS

The Long Route: A Lover's Landing Novella

The Stranger in the Woods: A Crimson Falls Novella

Made in the USA
Middletown, DE
18 October 2024